QUEEN OF
DRAGONS

M. A. Valdellon

Published by M. A. Valdellon
www.melissavaldellon.com

Cover design by Elena Lavrova

ISBN-13: 978-0692990896
ISBN-10: 0692990895

Let me embrace thee, sour adversity, for wise men say it is the wisest course.

- *William Shakespeare*

CONTENTS

1

Fall 1998

She stared at the building looming just in front of her. Three stories full of people she didn't know and wasn't sure she could bring herself to risk caring about, her heart still miles away with the people she had left behind. She was so deep in her thoughts that she barely acknowledged her father, who was wishing her luck on her first day from where he sat in the car. She was still so torn with the recent move to a place she couldn't call home yet. Sure, she understood the circumstances, but to just pack up and leave everything behind so quickly… A few tears gathered in the corners of her eyes, but she blinked them back. After all, she was a transfer student here. Why give her fellow students a reason to take note of her so soon? So she straightened up, clutched her things closely, and became one with the crowd of students that flowed into the building.

She could hear people calling out, lockers squeaking open and slamming shut, teachers and students all getting reacquainted after a summer away from each other. If anything else, she was glad to start over at the beginning of the year here at the same time as everyone else, especially given the short notice of their move. She hung onto that positive thought as she tried to find her locker in the midst of the growing groups of people around her. She was so intent on ignoring the commotion around her that it wasn't until she was on the floor, a few of her belongings scattered about, that she'd even realized she'd run into anybody. It was a classic new student move, and she knew that the moment would probably be funny in hindsight, but for now, she tried to hide her embarrassment and the curious looks being directed her way as she bent to retrieve her belongings.

When the girl finally straightened, she found herself looking into a pair of deep blue eyes. "Here, you dropped this also."

She looked over and saw that the guy was holding another of her notebooks. "Uhh, yeah. Thanks," she mumbled, smiling tentatively as she took the notebook and began to move away.

"Hey, wait," the guy called.

She hesitated, wondering what he could possibly want and inwardly cursing her luck. Right now, she just wanted to be alone with her thoughts and not be in the presence of this guy. A quick assessment of her surroundings had made it obvious enough that he was popular, guessing by the number of people hanging with him. 'And not only popular but cute too,' she thought, recalling also the cheerleader that had had her arm wrapped around his waist before the collision.

"You're new here, aren't you?" he asked.

"Is it that obvious?" she responded, trying her best to avoid his eyes.

"Well, you did seem a little lost. Want me to help

you find your locker?"

"No, that's okay. Really, I can find it on my own."

"I insist."

She hesitated a moment longer before deciding to follow the first good feeling she'd had that morning. "That would be a big help actually. But only if you insist," she added, smiling a little more as she looked up at him again.

"Consider it done. Let me get my stuff." She watched as he retrieved his backpack from a pile on the floor near his friends and said his good-byes before turning back to her. "So what's your locker number anyway?"

She told him the number and he nodded.

"This way then," he said, glancing back the way she had just come. He led her past the stairs she had come up, to the east side of the building. "Well what do you know? I thought the number was familiar. This used to be my friend's locker."

"Oh really?" She looked up at him.

"Yup. He graduated last year."

"What a coincidence."

"Sure is. Anyway, why don't you put your stuff away and then let's get you to your first class."

"Um, no, that's all right. I mean, thanks for your help, but I'm sure I can find it on my own."

"Just like you found your locker?" he teased.

She blushed lightly. "I would have found it eventually."

"I know, but I still would like to take you to your class."

"If you insist..."

"I do. Just get what you need and let's go. By the

way, my name is Damon."

"I'm-." She got cut off when a loud voice boomed out to her companion, easily being heard above the rest of the hallway noise.

"Damon!"

She watched as a huge guy came over to slap Damon on the back. "This is it! Ready for our last year?"

"You bet Riley," he laughed as she turned to her locker to put some things away and let them alone a moment. The moment passed quickly though. As she heard Damon say he'd see Riley later, she hurried to shut her locker door. "Well, ready to go?"

"Might as well." She couldn't help hide the grimace that crossed her face.

He gave a laugh and she found herself smiling back, despite her embarrassment as people turned to stare in her direction again. Thankfully, the warning bell rang at that moment and Damon led her through the crowds of people once she told him what her first class was.

Moments later, they were standing in front of her classroom. The teacher was greeting his students as they came in and he smiled a friendly smile to her as she went in. "Mr. West! How's it going?"

The girl looked back toward the door even as she found an open seat for her to settle into and caught Damon and her teacher clasping hands. "Oh, you know Damon. The same old stuff like always. How have you been? My class just hasn't been the same without you, you know."

"So you keep telling me," he laughed.

"Well it's true. No one else has had the guts to try and talk back to me about football. Anyway, shouldn't you be heading off to class now?"

"Naw, it's all right. I'm just right next door."

"With Ms. Sherwood?"

"Yup. I just wanted to say hi and make sure this one got here safely," he nodded to her and she quickly ducked her eyes, trying to not make it obvious that she'd been listening to them.

"Always so considerate, Damon. Now go, I'll talk to you some more later. The bell's about to ring."

"Sure thing, Mr. West. See you later. You too, umm..." He faltered when he looked back at her. "I'm sorry. I don't think I quite caught your name."

She smiled at the guilty look he suddenly had. "It's Sharon."

His smile returned. "Right. Nice meeting you, Sharon."

"Yeah, it was nice..." she trailed off when he dashed out of the doorway and ducked himself into his own classroom, finding a vacant seat in the back just as the bell rang. She looked up at the teacher and found him smiling at her kindly, a twinkle in his eyes. Sharon blushed and focused on opening a fresh notebook for her first class.

'All right, fifteen minutes in and so far, I haven't made a complete fool of myself, though I have a sneaky suspicion I'm not doing so well in keeping myself out of the gossip mill. Still, I think I can do this, especially with Damon being so nice and all...' And just like that, Sharon shut her feelings down as a feeling of dread washed over her. 'Damon was just being nice and he's most likely taken already, probably by that cheerleader. And even if he isn't, then he probably has a lot of others to choose from. No, he'd have nothing to do with me, especially if he ever found out about-'

She quietly exhaled a sharp breath, effectively stopping herself from finishing that thought. With that, Sharon turned her attention to the teacher who was handing out a class syllabus, losing herself in the teacher's introductions.

2

"So who was the new girl? She was kinda cute."

Damon turned around and spotted Riley and some of their other friends coming towards him. He smiled a greeting and watched as they all sat down at the table for lunch. "All I know is that her name is Sharon and that she's in our class. She had Mr. West first period this morning."

"That's her name? I'm in that class with her. She seems pretty quiet," Vin, one of the other guys, said.

"And how could you tell? Mr. West lectures the entire time, even on the first day. When would you guys be able to talk?" Riley teased.

"Point taken," Vin replied, smiling and lifting his arms up in mock surrender. "I'm just saying she seems to be the quiet type. She didn't talk to anyone after class. Just kinda left and kept to herself, you know?"

"With only five minutes to get to the next class, what else would you expect of her? She's new and still finding her way around," Damon pointed out.

He shrugged. "She could have asked someone for help, I dunno."

"Hey guys. Hey Damon."

He turned toward the new voice and smiled easily. "Hey Ana. How were your first couple of classes?" Damon asked as he scooted his chair over a bit for the smiling brunette so she could move a chair over to the table.

"Same old, same old," she smiled back, pushing her thick shoulder length brown hair back behind her shoulders. "English is going to be a bore and so will calculus. You'd think we could get cooler classes our senior year."

Damon laughed. "You're the one who decided to take those classes, Ana. No one said you couldn't take it easy your last year."

"And if I took it easy, I wouldn't be getting anywhere after I graduate. Thanks but no thanks. I have some big dreams to reach. I'll find some fun one way or another."

"Well, the welcome dance is tomorrow, and if I'm not mistaken, you and I are going."

"You and I are required to go help set up as upstanding members of our student council," she said, drawing herself up to sit tall, though her serious words and posture were undermined by her laughter. "You call that fun?"

"The dancing part that happens after the setting up, yes. I think that'll be fun."

"Always trying to find the best out of every situation, aren't you?" she smiled.

"Of course I try. If I didn't, I'd go crazy," he smiled back. "Besides, you know you think the same as I do."

"Any more similar, and you'd think we hadn't just grown up all these years together."

A few feet away, Sharon was finally making it to the cafeteria. She'd wanted to talk to her last teacher a little bit after class about some of the extra work she'd have to do on the side to make sure she was on par with everyone else in the class. She had tried her best to stall as long as possible; lunch was next and she didn't want to deal with the looks and whispering that she could imagine was happening around her. Her teacher, however, had class after lunch and needed to get some last minute things together and had sent Sharon on her way. Now, her eyes looked around for a place to sit and found a spot at the end of a long table nearby. With notebook and lunch in hand, she made her way to the table and sat down, trying her best to ignore the curious glances coming her way. 'Let them look,' she thought. 'Soon enough, the novelty will wear off, and I'll just be the quiet one who just likes to keep to herself.' She tried to let that thought sink in, hanging onto the idea that in keeping her distance, she'd be safe…

She took the pencil from behind her ear and flipped another notebook to a clean page. Almost unconsciously, she drew her legs up and folded them underneath her as she concentrated on the blank page in front of her. She was already scratching away when she started to eat her sandwich.

"Hey, isn't that the new girl?"

Damon looked over to where one of the guys was pointing and spotted her only a couple of tables away working on something in a notebook as she ate her lunch. Both he and Vin nodded. "That's her all right."

"What's she working on? She can't be doing homework already."

"After only two classes? I would hope not, and if

she is, remind me to try and transfer out of those classes if I have the same teachers as her."

"You guys are so lazy!" Ana exclaimed, laughing.

"Come on! We have our dumb jock image to maintain here Ana. Give us a break," Riley smiled from across the table.

"And you guys play it up so well."

"What? And you don't act the part of ditzy cheerleader every now and again?"

Ana gave a dramatic flip of her hair. "What, me? Of course not."

A sudden burst of laughter managed to cut through Sharon's concentration, and she blinked a couple of times to re-orient herself. She looked up towards the source and found Damon a few feet away at a round table. He was surrounded by a bunch of people she could only assume to be fellow football players, spotting Riley in among the crowd. And there was the girl she'd seen with them that morning too, laughing right along with them. A small pang hit her. 'I miss that, laughing and hanging out. I miss my friends. I wonder what they're doing back home…' She sighed and looked down at her notebook again and frowned. 'Stop it, Sharon. I know I wish I had had more time to say good-bye but this is your home now. You can't go back even if you wanted to.'

She glanced up again and found Damon looking directly at her. She blinked, surprised. He smiled and waved hi. Automatically, she shyly waved back, smiling a little bit in return before turning away again.

"Come on, Ana. I think we have to exercise our

role as welcoming committee," Damon said, drawing himself up and beckoning the girl to follow before anyone could protest, all the while still smiling. Once he'd reached their destination, he pulled up a couple of extra seats for Ana and himself. "Hey Sharon. How's your first day so far?" he asked as he straddled his chair to face her.

She took a quick breath and braced herself, already recognizing that voice. "Uhh, it's all been all right so far I guess," she answered, smiling a little bit as she looked up. "How about you?"

He shrugged. "Not too bad actually. Anyway, Sharon, this is Ana. Ana, this is Sharon."

"Nice to meet you, Sharon," Ana smiled warmly, sticking out a hand.

"Nice to meet you too," she replied, taking the offered hand and shaking it.

"Anyway, as part of the unofficial welcoming committee, Ana and I just wanted to let you know that the school's welcome back dance is being held tomorrow night. If you don't have any other plans, we'd love it if you could come."

"Oh, I don't know. My family just moved in a few days ago, and we're still trying to get settled in."

"Oh, I see," Ana replied. "Well, if you decide you need a break, you know where to go then. And definitely let us know if you or your family needs any help with anything, settling in, finding the best local places to shop or eat or hang out, whatever."

Sharon smiled wider this time, feeling genuine warmth come up. "Thanks for the offer Ana. That'd be nice."

"Anytime. That's what we're here for."

Just then, the warning bell rang, signaling that class was going to start again in five minutes. With a quick smile and wave good-bye, Damon and Ana rushed back to get their backpacks as Sharon stood up and started heading back to the main building. She looked down at her schedule and smiled, seeing that her elective class was next. She made a left and found herself in a different wing of the building. She found the room number and put her hand on the doorknob.

"Sharon!"

Her hand dropped back, and she turned to see Damon rushing to catch up with her. "Hey. Following me now?"

"It depends," he smiled, catching up to her. "Do you have art with Mr. Flynn next?" She nodded. "Then that'd be a yes, I'm following you," he winked, opening the door for her and letting her go in ahead of him. She laughed easily and the two found a couple of seats next to the windows.

As the teacher handed out his syllabus and went through it, Damon found himself glancing over to Sharon. She looked a bit more relaxed now compared to the morning. The soft afternoon light was coming from behind them and she was leaning over with her chin in the palm of her left hand. For the first time that day, he allowed himself to take a good look at her. She was dressed casually – no impressing anyone on the first day obviously, and he figured she was trying to just blend in between how she was dressed and how she'd been acting so far. A worn in, comfortable pair of jeans hugged her legs on top of the sandals she wore. She had been wearing a light jacket earlier to fight the morning chill but now that it was afternoon, the jacket was on the floor resting on her bag. On top, she wore a simple black tank top. Her hair flowed past her shoulders in a loose ponytail and it looked to be as dark and rich as Ana's, but while Ana's hair was naturally on the curly side, Sharon's was straight. He noticed that she was wearing little flower earrings that sparkled a little in the light. He turned to her face and noticed that unlike many of the girls in their class, she wore little make-up, just a little bit of lip-gloss. Right now, her mouth was turned up a little at the sides, smiling a little at the teacher's attempt to crack a joke. Her dark brown eyes were focused on their teacher, Mr. Flynn, and still lit up with a little bit of the laughter from before.

'Riley was right. She is cute,' he thought to himself as the class finally broke up to begin working on their first of a series of sketches they'd create. He stretched his arms overhead for a moment before staring at the blank piece of paper in front of him. 'Come on Damon. Do you really have to think about this?' Grinning a little to himself, he started working.

Sharon had pulled out her sketchbook from earlier and was concentrating on her work. She took pride in her artwork, knowing how much she needed and benefited from this creative outlet. She concentrated on the portrait in front of her and, for a moment, let go of the hurt and pain, the anger and sadness that she knew she still needed to process.

"Good job Sharon. That looks really good."

Damon looked up from his paper and turned to his left where Mr. Flynn was critiquing Sharon's work. "Thank you," he heard her say before Mr. Flynn came over to his easel.

"Really Damon?" he smiled, taking in the view in front of him.

"What can I say, Mr. Flynn? I'm a Dragon through and through," he grinned back, referring to their school mascot. As the teacher moved on, Damon stole a look at Sharon's work and caught himself whistling. "He's right, you know."

Sharon looked up. "Hmm?"

"Your drawing," he answered, pointing to her sketch of a girl's face that was half hidden by cloth. Well, it was more of a girl's eyes than the face actually. While there was a basic outline of a head and a few light lines to indicate the nose and lips, she'd worked hard on the eyes first, getting them to stand out almost life-like from the stark white of the paper. "It's really good."

She blushed lightly. "Thanks Damon," she replied. Just then, the bell rang, and the class began gathering itself together to pour back out into the halls. "I guess I'll see you later then," she said as the two started to go opposite directions upon leaving the room.

"Definitely. Have a good rest of the first day," he smiled.

"Thanks. You too," she waved before losing herself once again to the mass of people.

3

"Hi sweetie. How was school today?"

Sharon shrugged off her backpack in the hallway and went into the kitchen. There, she found her mother standing on a chair cleaning out the cupboards with some rags. "Hi mom," she said, reaching up to give her mother a hug. "School was fine. Better than expected. Need some help?"

"Oh no dear. Don't worry about it. I'm sure you have some homework to be doing anyway, right?"

"Nothing that won't take me more than a few minutes. Here, let me take that. You go take a break," she answered, taking the rag from her mother's hand and beckoning for her to come down off the chair.

"Well, if you insist," her mom answered, wiping her forehead a little bit. "Thanks. A break does sound rather good right now. Let me know if you need anything. I think I'm going to go lay down for a minute."

"No problem." She watched as her mother left the room before turning back to the cupboards. For the next couple of hours, she scrubbed and cleaned the kitchen. And when she was done, she found herself nodding in satisfaction. 'Finally. Now we can go grocery shopping instead of having to eat out so much.' She retreated back into the living room, picked up her backpack from the hallway, and moved on to her room.

She paused in her doorway, taking in the simple room. Her bed rested against one wall, her nightstand beside it with a clock, lamp, and a couple of pictures with her family and friends. Against the other wall were her desk and a couple of small bookshelves. The last corner of her room was left for her media collection and a few of her artwork pieces, along with the beanbag chair she used whenever she just needed to relax and draw.

She headed to that last corner now to turn on some low music, mindful that her mom was probably still resting down the hall. Then she walked over to her desk and emptied out her backpack, placing books and notebooks onto one shelf. One look over to the clock told her that she had another good hour or so before they were likely to eat, so she took the top book off the stack and started reading for her English class. The words blurred together in front of her, however, and she found her mind going elsewhere.

Seeing that she wasn't going to get anywhere soon with her homework, she moved from her desk to her beanbag, taking some stationary and a pen with her. *Dear Kelly,* she wrote after settling in.

Has it already been more than a week since I last saw you? Time has flown by on my side what with all the moving in and out and stuff, but don't get me wrong. I miss you and the others terribly. It's not fair that I had to leave so soon after all this happened. Life just seems so bleak without you around to talk to and tell all my problems to. What's been going on since I left?

How are you? Are you any better? …sigh… You don't know how bad I feel for all of this, for going so soon after leaving the hospital, for not listening to you sooner… But I'm out now, right? And you guys are safe. And he's finally where he belongs… Who knew that things would go this far or be this crazy? Still, as you always say, there is a point to life and what happens in it. I just have to figure out what it is, right?

So today was the first day of school here. Nothing happened out of the extraordinary. Dad dropped me off. I had trouble finding my locker and ended up literally running into this cute guy. Before you start screaming though, I should tell you that I think he has a girlfriend already, some cheerleader. He's a football player. And his name is Damon. He seems super nice so far. He helped me find my locker and my first class. He and the girl I think is his girlfriend (her name's Ana) invited me to go to the welcome dance that I guess is happening tomorrow night but we'll see. They're both nice, but I don't know if I'm ready to head out into the social world yet. But if it helps, Damon's in my art class. And he sat next to me today. Wipe that smirk off your face and stop laughing K. Nothing's going to happen, at least not yet. I think I've had enough of taking fate into my own hands and just want to go along with the ride, at least for now.

Sharon paused and stared down at the sheets of stationary down in her lap, her pen lightly tapping the clipboard in time with the music as she thought of what to say next.

Okay, so I lied. You of all people know that I am anything but the sit around and wait for something happen type of girl. At the same time, can you blame me for being a little jumpy right now? It was certainly strange eating on my own for once during lunch. When was the last time that happened, huh? Not even in grade school, but now? I know I wasn't helping by actually choosing to be on my own, but it's the price I'm going to pay to be safe. I don't want to get hurt again, physically, emotionally… I couldn't do that to myself, much less make anyone else go through it again (aka, parental units here). It was hard enough the first time.

But watching Damon and his group of friends at lunch… Seeing them all having a good time and goofing off like we used to do… I admit that I miss the company. I know there's no rule against me having friends. That'd probably be the best thing I could do for myself right now, get new friends. The thought scares me though. Who can I trust? I don't know a single soul here – a good thing for the anonymity I'm thinking about adopting, but I'm not sure if I could ever get used to it.

I know what you're thinking. Whatever happened to the Sharon you used to know, right? Heh, I think the popular, self-assured girl you knew got killed that night, if only figuratively. Damn it, Kelly, do you think this cynicism will stay? I hope not, but the memories keep coming back. I hate it, but that's the reason anonymity looks good right now. I just don't know what to do. This holding back isn't like me at all, I know it, but I can't just be myself right now. It makes me too vulnerable. It'll put me in the spotlight, which is probably not the best thing for me right now. Who could have thought I would ever be reduced to something like this?

Okay, I've got to stop this train of thought. It isn't exactly the most heartwarming thing you've read, I know, and I'm sorry. It's just that I've got this all pent up inside me and I need to let it out. My parents don't really want to talk about it, and there's no one else I can trust but you to hear me out anyway. Some things can never take the place of a best friend, you know? Anyway, I think it really is time for me to end this letter as it's almost dinnertime. I guess I'll talk to you soon though, all right? Take care of yourself chica, and I'll hopefully be seeing you sometime soon.

Always,
Sharon

Sharon pulled out an envelope and sealed her letter inside. Ignoring the pain in her hand that had come from writing for so long, she forced herself to hold onto the pen just long enough to address the envelope to her best friend before sitting back and flexing her stiff fingers. She allowed herself a moment longer to close her eyes and imagine her best friend's reaction when she got the letter. A small smile formed and she sighed. 'I certainly hope things get better for all of us soon,' she thought as she stood up and made her way back out to the kitchen to help with dinner.

4

The next day, Sharon found herself doodling in the margins of her test as she waited for time to be called. Her English teacher had asked Sharon before class if she had felt okay about taking the summer reading test along with the rest of the class even though she was new. Sharon had said she was fine with it. It had helped that one of the books off the list was one she herself had read during the spring at her former high school.

So now she sat, sketching out small scenes on the sides of her paper as she waited for the last five minutes to pass by until she could go out and eat her lunch, paying no mind to the almost frantic scribbling of her classmates. Her short essays had been done for quite some time, the work still fresh in her memory.

She cocked her head to one side as she looked down to what she was drawing. 'A castle and a dragon? Of all the stuff I could be drawing now… But it's not because of him,' she tried to tell herself but instead gave a small sigh. 'Oh, who are you trying to fool Sharon?' She blushed, knowing full well why she was drawing the mythical creatures in the first place. 'Damon…'

Down the hall, Damon was jotting down notes in his physics class, listening as Mr. Plopper finished off his quick review of the atom and bonds. 'Man, if only the class would stay this easy,' he thought to himself while trying to ignore the urge to start packing his things up before the bell had rung. 'Your luck for being in the honors system Damon. Just be thankful that at least there was an easy lecture to be had with Plopper. From what everyone else has said, there will be no more freebies in this class.'

The bell rang and he slammed his notebook shut, barely paying attention to his teacher as he reminded his students to do the reading for the following week. He stuffed his backpack with his things and easily swung it onto his shoulder as he walked out the door. He glanced up and down the hall quickly to see whom he could find and spotted Sharon heading his way. Smiling, he fell into step beside her. "How's it going? Are you all settled in yet?"

Sharon turned and smiled up at him. "For the most part, I guess. Finding my way around isn't as hard as I thought it would be."

"With a small high school like this, it'd be hard to get lost," he grinned back. "So how you managed to not find your locker without help yesterday is beyond me."

"Please Damon," she said, rolling her eyes. "I was barely in the building for more than two minutes! Give a girl a break!"

"Only if you go to the welcome back dance tonight. That can be your break."

"I don't know…"

"Oh come on Sharon!" he said as they reached her locker. "It'll be fun."

"I don't know if I'd have fun without knowing anyone there…"

"But you know me. And Ana will be there too!"

An indescribable look crossed her face for a fleeting moment, but she turned away into her locker before he could interpret the look. "Oh boy, two people! That's really knowing everybody."

"Your sarcasm has no power over me," he joked. "Besides, you can't get to know people if you're going to be spending all of your time hiding, Sharon. Give us a chance."

She looked sideways over to where he was casually leaning on the locker next to hers, as if this were something they'd been doing all along. "What makes you think I'm hiding?"

He shrugged. "The fact that you were sitting by yourself at lunch yesterday maybe? Or the fact that I haven't seen you talk to anyone besides your teachers or myself?"

"You're just catching me at weird times."

"Am I?" He gave her a pointed look.

"No," she answered honestly as she shut her locker door and moved with him towards his locker.

"So tell me Sharon, are you hiding?"

"I'm not necessarily hiding per se. I just don't want to gain attention. That's all."

"Sorry, but you're the new girl in town. That kind of warrants you attention right there."

"Not bad attention, I hope."

"Of course not. People are just curious about you, that's all. The fact that you aren't opening up to people makes them wonder about you."

"I don't freely give when I haven't been asked,"

she smiled. "And no one has really bothered to ask. Still, you have me wondering."

"About…" he asked as he opened his locker and began transferring his books to and from his backpack.

"You." He paused a moment to look at her before deciding it was best to just let her continue. "You aren't one to just sit back and judge me before getting to know me, are you?"

He smiled over at her. "You really do have a way with words, don't you?"

"I believe in being as honest and open as I can be, you know?"

He nodded. "Very true."

"So you haven't answered me."

"Repeat the question then," he smiled.

"What makes you any different from all the other people? What is it about you that makes you actually brave enough to talk to me?"

He laughed. "Look at me Sharon! Guys twice your size are scared of me! Why should I be scared of talking to someone like you?"

"Seriously!" she laughed along with him as the two walked outdoors for lunch.

He chuckled. "Seriously then? How about I grew up with the firm belief that people miss out if one just assumes things about others." He glanced over at her and found a small, surprised look on her face. He nodded. "My mother always says that there is more to people than just their looks or whatever and she hasn't been wrong thus far. People always have their unique history, their own minds behind their actions, and I try to remember that before making any sort of judgment."

"I'm impressed. I never knew that a football player could be so thoughtful."

"What did I just tell you about people being more than what they seem?"

"I know, I know. I'm kidding," she laughed.

Damon found himself laughing with her. "Come on. I think there are some people I should introduce you to. No hiding now."

She nodded. "All right. No hiding… For now at least," she grinned.

He just shook his head and took her hand to lead the way.

As simple as the gesture had been, there was no denying the shock she got as they walked on hand in hand. 'Okay, this is definitely new.' She also couldn't help but note how naturally their hands seemed to fit together too, and that observation shook her more than she wanted to admit. 'I don't think I've ever felt electricity like that before…'

Damon was glad that he'd been slightly ahead of her so she couldn't see the surprise on his face when he had grabbed her hand. He had meant the gesture out of friendship. Why then did he feel like this? 'Electricity in just holding hands?' He opened the door to the cafeteria and let go of her hand to allow her to enter first. He mentally shook himself. 'Okay Damon. Obviously, skin is bad right now.' He smiled at her, hiding his thoughts as he drew her along, this time guiding her along by placing his hand on her opposite shoulder and leading her to the group.

'As if this were any better,' she thought to

herself, feeling the warmth of his hand through the thin material of her top. 'What the…?' She gave a slight sigh when they reached his table and he let her go. 'Though, if I'm honest with myself, is this a sigh of relief or a sigh of already missing his touch?'

"Hey you two," Ana smiled, glancing up from a notebook and scooting her chair a little bit to give the two room at the table. "Classes going okay so far?"

"Please Ana!" Riley exclaimed from where he sat next to her. "Can we talk about something besides classes for once?"

"And what else are we going to talk about? How you guys are going to lose your first game?"

"Low blow," he replied, smiling. "You have no right to talk to us like that. Especially in front of our star quarterback here," he said, indicating to Damon. "Then again, if we do lose, now it's going to be all your fault now that you said it."

"No way," she laughed. "It's not going to happen because you guys are too good. Still, here you go anyway," she said, knocking on the table before them. "Better? It's wood."

"Only slightly," he grinned back.

Sharon poked Damon in the side. "Quarterback?"

He grinned. "You didn't ask."

"And you didn't tell," she grinned back.

"So are you just going to keep her to yourself or are you going to introduce us D?"

Damon glanced up and smiled. "My apologies. Everyone, this is Sharon. Sharon, this is my group of friends. You've met Ana. Next to her is Riley, Vin,…"

- - -

It was the last class for the day, and halfway through it, the speakers went on throughout the school.

"May I have your attention, please? May I have your attention, please?"

Sharon and the rest of her class stopped with their activity to listen to the announcement.

"This is your public relations officer Hilary Benton speaking. As part of your ASB council, I'd personally like to welcome all of you to a new school year. To help kick things off right, we are gathering you all together for our first general assembly of the year. Teachers, please accompany your class to the main gym after I have called your room number. Students, please leave your belongings…"

Sharon ignored the rest of the message as she and her classmates started packing their things together.

After her class had been called, she found herself going along with the steady stream of people heading toward the gym. A small bit of worry entered her stomach when she realized she had no one to sit with. Damon had been right; she hadn't made any effort to get to know anybody yet. She blamed it on the sudden move and the fact that she was still getting herself situated. She needed to find herself first before she could feel completely comfortable in her new surroundings.

'It helps that Damon's being so nice. And his group of friends seems to be all right so far too.

Speaking of…'

Sharon craned her neck around, trying to find a familiar face in the crowd and finding none. Then again, the walls were all just a sea of unfamiliar faces to her, and she ended up just drifting towards one wall and taking a seat in the bleachers next to a girl who smiled kindly at her before turning back to talk to her friends.

After the last couple of classes had settled in, a girl took the podium toward the front of the gym and got everyone's attention. 'Hey, isn't that…'

"Welcome everyone to our first assembly of the year! How's everyone doing today?" An answer of cheers and whistles came in reply. She laughed. "That's great. I'm glad to see all your smiling faces here today as well. Anyway, as many of you know, my name is Ana, and I'm going to be your ASB president for the next school year. One of the purposes of today's assembly is to introduce you to your board members for the coming year. Frosh, your board elections take place in two weeks, including those positions for ASB senators. If you're interested in running, please come see myself or anyone else on student council ASAP for your applications. Sophs, your class council is made of representatives…"

Ana introduced the members of the sophomore, junior, and senior class councils starting from class representatives up to the president of each class. Sharon sat back and watched as the student council members each left the main lobby of the gym and made their entrance, not really paying attention even as the rest of Ana's own council started making their ways into the gym. There were the public relations officer, the senate leader, spirit commissioners... Sharon didn't care until she heard Ana finishing up the list with: "Vice-president Damon, and me, your associated student body president." Ana smiled as the rest of the school clapped and cheered as Damon took Ana's arm in his and the two joined the student council on the floor and broke into a skit to liven up the crowd and introduce the rest of the school to each of their different personalities.

By the time they were done, the school was cheering quite loudly, Sharon right along with them, easily getting caught up in the school spirit. The group took their bows as Ana went to the podium again, still laughing. "Thank you. On behalf of the student council, I would like to wish you all a happy new school year and promise you that this year will be full of fun and great times. To kick it off, tonight starting at seven right here, we're having our annual welcome back dance. It's only five bucks and believe me, it'll be worth it. The theme tonight is tropical paradise so come on by, have some fun, and show your school spirit. Thanks everybody!"

There was some more cheering as the student council gave their final bows and cleared the floor, leaving the podium so the principal could say a few words before she dismissed the school for the day.

5

"Don't you want to go to the dance tonight Sharon?"

"To be honest mom, I don't know. I'm not sure I'd feel comfortable knowing only a handful of people there. And besides, I should stay here and help you with the chores."

"Now this is a first. You volunteering to stay home on a Friday night? What is the world coming to?" Her father laughed.

Sharon blushed a little. "I just don't feel right about going out so soon after we've moved in, that's all."

"Don't go making excuses where there aren't any dear. You know as well as we do that you really want to go. Personally, I think that it'd be a good thing for you to go," her mom stated.

"Really? You never liked me going out before. What makes it different here?" She caught the look that her parents gave each other and waited patiently for an explanation.

"The difference here is that he's not here to ruin it for you. Frankly, we didn't mind you going out when it was with Kelly or your other friends. It was just him we didn't like. He was changing you, controlling you. You weren't you when he was around. You know that, right?" Her mom had come over and squeezed her hand, emphasizing her point.

Sharon nodded and sighed. "I know," she answered softly, turning away slightly. "I just wish sometimes that things could have been different, you know? What if all this never happened?"

"Honey, everything happens for a reason. We can play the "what if" game all we want, but there really isn't any point in going what if."

The seventeen-year-old nodded. "But I still don't know if I feel right going. You're right. A big part of me wants to go tonight. I want to have fun and forget about everything that's happened. At the same time…" She trailed off, sighing. "I just don't know."

"Well then think about it. It doesn't start for another couple of hours so you've got some time. Just…" Her mom shrugged and sighed. "Don't forget that we want you to be happy too, and your father and I are sure that shutting yourself up in your room isn't the way to do that." Sharon nodded her understanding. "Good. Let us know if you need anything, okay?"

"Thanks. You're the best," she said, giving them each a hug before going to her room. She quietly shut the door behind her so she could turn on her radio. After she had done just that, she found herself taking out a scrapbook and settling down into the beanbag chair. She flipped it open to the first page and was greeted with the smiling faces of her closest friends.

She sighed as she flipped through the pages. 'Has it really been almost two weeks now? It seems like it's been so much longer than that with all that's been going on… And that's all the more reason for you to move on too, Sharon. Nothing's holding you back. The past is past. Your parents are trying to make things better for you. They want you to live. You want to live. You knew it wasn't going to be easy but you've got to do it all the same. Baby steps Sharon. That's all there is to it...'

As Sharon continued to contemplate whether or not to go to the dance, Damon found himself still at school. There had been a quick student council meeting after the assembly to discuss a few last minute preparations for the welcome dance. As usual, Ana had taken the meeting entirely into her hands and made sure that everything was on track for that night. 'If not for her though, no doubt we probably would have just sat around and wasted time,' he thought to himself when he waved good-bye to the others and rushed off to the football field for their first practice of the school year.

Once he pulled the practice jersey over his head and stepped onto the field, all thoughts of the dance or anything else fled his mind. He spent the next couple of hours grunting and sweating, going through some old plays with his team after stretching and going through some basic drills. Once they had refreshed their minds with a couple of the old plays though, the light atmosphere changed to one more serious as they began to alter little details to their plays here and there to see what worked until their coach finally called it quits for the night. Damon joined the others in giving a sigh of relief and sprinted to the locker room to towel off quickly.

He eyed the clock and groaned. It was already

after five o'clock. With a rushed good-bye to his teammates, he flew out of the changing area and got into his car. Why he hadn't bothered to just bring his dance clothes along with him when he left that morning, knowing that he would be rushed if he tried to go home between practice and the dance set up, escaped him. All he knew was that he had roughly forty-five minutes to go home, take a shower, get changed, try to eat some dinner, and come straight back to school to help set up the gym.

"And this is just week one. Whoever said that senior year was supposed to be easy must have been crazy," he muttered under his breath as he raced out of his car and into the house. "Hi Mom and Dad! I'm home!" he yelled out as he took the stairs two at a time up to the second floor of the house. "Hey Squirt," he said, ruffling the hair of his eleven-year-old brother as he rushed by. "Hi Ros," he greeted his little sister, bending down for a moment to give her a hug.

"Eww!" she squealed, laughing as she pushed him away. "You're stinky!"

"I love you too," he smiled as he finally made it to his room and jumped into the shower.

Twenty-five minutes later, he was downing the last of his meal and rushing back up the stairs to brush his teeth one last time. In the bathroom, he took one last look at himself in the mirror as he ran a comb through his hair a final time. Satisfied with what he saw, he ran back down the stairs, said good-bye to his family (who were all at the table just about to start eating their dinner), and jumped back into his car to head back to school.

He stepped inside to find the DJs already in the middle of setting up their equipment at the other end of the gym. With a quick glance around, he spotted Ana and made his way over. "Miss me much?" he asked her, giving her a hug.

"Of course not!" she said, laughing as she pushed him off her. "Who would miss you?"

Damon mockingly placed his hands over his heart and moaned. "Ana, your words do hurt me so, especially when you know that I have missed you most dearly in the," he glanced down to his watch. "Two and three quarter hours since we last saw each other."

She laughed, shaking her head. "Stop groaning and start blowing. You're on balloon duty," she said, pointing to where a helium tank stood. "Here, take these." She gave him a few packs of balloons.

He grinned. "You want all of them done?"

She nodded. "Please. And when Stuart gets here, make sure he helps you out."

"Aye aye, Captain!" he saluted to her, ignoring how she rolled her eyes at him before turning away.

Ana glanced down at her watch. 'Half an hour until show time.' She looked down at the checklist in her hand and penciled in a check mark next to the balloons. 'All right, so where does that leave us? DJ's are here and getting ready, so that means Mr. Heusner already showed them where the outlets were so they're good. All right, music done. Refreshments…' Ana made her way towards another part of the gym where a few of the staff were setting up the soda and water. 'Cups, napkins, check and check. And they got ice and stuff, all right, good here.' She smiled and waved bye to them as she walked over to where the photographers were finishing setting up. 'All good there too,' she nodded to herself, smiling.

Ana went to the front of the gym. 'Cashier box, lists of students, highlighters, bracelets, scissors all here. Good.'

"Is everything okay, Ana?"

"Everything's looking great, Mrs. Faulkin," she turned, smiling at the student council moderator. "Everyone is pretty much getting the last of their things together. I think we'll be able to open the doors right on time."

"I'm impressed. It looks like you and this year's student council are off to a smooth, wonderful start."

"Let's just hope it stays that way."

"I'm sure you all can do it. Anyway, did you want to gather everyone up already? We've got about another twenty minutes before the doors open, and I think the photographers are set up for your pictures."

"Sounds great, Mrs. Faulkin," Ana answered, taking her leave. She walked back through the doors and into the gym, taking note of the decorations that had transformed the gym into a tropical paradise. Nodding to herself in satisfaction, she found herself linking her arm through Damon's, effectively distracting him from where he had been sitting with Stuart relaxing while she never missed a step. "Looks good guys," she said, seeing that all the balloons were finished. A few had been left to scatter the floor, those that hadn't been filled with the helium. A few hung from the backs of a few chairs. Damon had even let a few go so that they floated against the ceiling. All in all, they hadn't done a bad job of it. She smiled. "Student council members to the photo area! Sophomore council, you guys are up first!" she yelled in her best commanding voice.

Damon winced and plugged his ear. "Hello? I'm right here Ana!"

"I know that," she grinned back as the two led the group of students to the cameras.

Fifteen minutes later, Ana was dragging Damon along with her towards the front of the gym.

"What now?" he asked.

"I'm making you go to the bathroom now. You and I are on bracelet duty in about five minutes when we open the doors, and I don't want you to be making excuses and leaving me to do it all by myself," she said, giving him a look.

"But I thought Dorothy and Kent were doing that," he whined a little.

"Obviously, someone wasn't paying attention during the meeting. We went over this already. They're on ticket duty and we're doing bracelets."

"And that's why you're the president and not me. You always know what's going on, and I can count on you to tell me what I need to know."

"One of these days, I'm going to stop acting like your mother and just let you take over and get into trouble, you know that?" she asked, laughing as she practically shoved him into the guys' bathroom. "Don't fall in, all right?" she called in after him.

"Sure thing Ana!" she heard him call back to her.

- - -

Damon unconsciously nodded his head in time with the music that filtered in through the closed gym doors behind him. Forty-five minutes into the dance, he found himself alone in the lobby tidying things up. The number of people coming in had trickled down after half an hour, and no one else had come in for the past five minutes. He had encouraged Ana and the others to go on in ahead of him – he was all right with putting everything away. Ana had been hesitant at first. She trusted him, but she didn't want to leave him alone either. He had insisted in the end, however, knowing that she deserved to relax after all the hard work she'd done to get this thing organized.

So now he sat at a table, already having helped one of the teachers put the other away. The lists of the students were piled neatly on one corner of the surface, already sorted by class standing. The highlighters and leftover bracelets and tickets were already rubber banded together and lay on top of the sheets of paper. The only thing left for him to do was sort through the money – not like there was much for him to do there anyway. Kent and Dorothy had kept a neat cashier box and all he was really doing was counting up the money and logging it into the student funds book for Mrs. Faulkin. Damon quickly finished up his counting and logged in the last figure as he sang along with a little bit of the tune that he recognized in the background. Something about learning to live or love again…

A slight cough let him know he was no longer alone. Damon looked up and found himself staring into a familiar pair of brown eyes. He smiled. "Hey Sharon."

"Hi Damon," she said quietly, smiling back at him a little. "Is it too late for me to buy a ticket?"

"Not for you," he smiled warmly.

6

Sharon lay on her stomach on her bed, her feet up in the air swinging back and forth as she worked on her sketchbook. The radio played softly in the background. A slight knock on her door made her glance up and pause in her work. "Come in."

"Good morning, darling."

"Morning, Mom," she answered, raising herself up slightly to give her mother a kiss on the cheek as she sat down next to her on the bed.

"So how was the dance last night?"

Sharon grinned. "I'm surprised you didn't ask me this yesterday when I came home on my own."

"We figured it out that since you hadn't called by the time the dance ended that you had just gone out afterwards with your new friends for a little bit."

"So does that mean I'm not in trouble for not calling you?"

"I think that given the circumstances, we can relax things a little bit," she laughed. "Just don't make it a habit."

"I won't. As for your question, the dance was fun. I had a really good time," the younger female grinned.

"I'm glad. Did you meet any boys?"

It was Sharon's turn to laugh. "And I've been waiting for that one since I came home from school the first day!"

"We're just giving you time to adjust, that's all dear."

"I know, I know, but you've got to admit that this is all amusing for me too. I keep telling you both I'm okay but you still act, oh I don't know, differently."

"Honey, we're getting over what happened just like you. This will all take time."

"I know, but I really do insist that I'm getting better."

"We know," mother said to her daughter. "It's only been a few days but we can tell you're happier now than you have been for months. You have a bit of sparkle in your eyes that I missed," she added, tilting her daughter's chin up with a hand. "I'm just wondering if that's because there's already a new guy in your life or not."

"Mom!" she laughed. "I don't know who's worse when it comes to me and all the boys I'm supposedly after, you or Kelly. The world doesn't revolve around them!"

"It's Kelly's job as your best friend and my job as your mother to torment you about it, don't forget that."

"Gee, thanks, I'm feeling the love here," she smiled. "Can't I just be happy to be out of a situation and to know that everyone's okay now?"

"Sure! But… That sparkle tells me something else is up."

"Nothing is up," she replied.

"There is too!"

"No, there isn't!" Her mother gave her a pointed look though, and Sharon found herself ducking her head down a little and blushing. "Fine, I'm caught. There is this guy…"

"Aha! I knew it!"

"But I don't know if he likes me back or not!" she added in a rush.

"Well, did you talk to him about it?"

The younger of the two shook her head. "It's only been two days! I hardly say that's enough time to really get to know someone enough to be able to ask him if he's taken or not."

"Well what have you heard from the others? Surely you've learned some of the local gossip."

Sharon shifted her eyes. "Not really. I've been trying to keep to myself mostly and not get myself caught in all of that."

Her mother looked at her, a little surprise on her face. "Really? How come?"

Sharon shrugged. "I guess I'm just a little scared to talk to people now, or at least I'm trying to be more careful. Talking leads to opening up and I don't want to say certain things to the wrong people and have it spread out before I can figure out who to trust or not yet. And in the meantime, I don't want to hear stuff being talked about behind my back, you know?"

"Dear, you know that you have control only over what you say. Other people… Well, you can't please everybody. They will interpret everything and say whatever they want anyway."

"True…"

"Well no use worrying now about it. It's the weekend. And in any case, I'm sure it will all turn out well in the end. Just take things one step at a time."

"I know. It's just that last night, I had a lot of fun. I don't want anything to jeopardize that," she replied, thinking back to the night before and giving a little sigh as she remembered it.

Sharon was sitting at a table with a few of Damon's friends, laughing at something Riley had said. They had taken a break from the dancing and had decided to sit out a couple of songs for a breather. When the up-tempo music changed to a slow song however, most of them left the table to go back onto the dance floor. Sharon sat there a moment longer, playing with the shell necklace that hung around her neck while she watched the couples sway in time with the music until she noticed that someone was standing next to her.

"Please don't tell me you want to just sit there when there's a perfectly good song playing," Vin said, smiling down at her.

"I don't know Vin. I think this is a couple's only song."

"Dance with me then," he said, offering his hand out to her. "Please?"

She bit her lip, smiling as she placed her hand in his. She allowed him to lead her onto the dance floor and then linked her arms around his neck when they found a suitable spot. She felt his arms settle themselves comfortably around her waist and she relaxed, allowing herself to enjoy the moment.

"There now. Isn't this better than sitting all alone at a table?"

She smiled. "Much better. Thank you for asking me to dance."

"You're welcome. We wouldn't want you to be bored during your first dance here now, would we?"

She laughed. "No, now that would be a tragedy, but for who, I don't know."

He joined in her laughter. "What can I say? It's a small enough town and we try to take care of our own here."

"I appreciate it. You and your friends have really made me feel welcome here these last couple of days."

"Then we're doing our job right," he grinned.

The two didn't say anything else as the song concluded and another slow ballad started. The two continued to dance together and she took the liberty to see who else was around them. She spotted Riley a few feet away with another girl in his arms. The couple was talking to another pair whom she recognized as part of Damon's group as well.

Sharon shifted her gaze and found it settling on Damon, where he and Ana were dancing off to one side of the floor a little isolated from everyone else. She remembered the electricity she had felt earlier that day when he had touched her. 'Such an innocent touch…' A small pit formed in her stomach when she saw him leaning down close to whisper something into Ana's ear. She couldn't quite control the sigh that escaped her and Vin noticed. "Something wrong Sharon?"

"Huh?" she asked, quickly looking back up into her partner's face. "Oh, no. Nothing's wrong."

He tilted his head to the side a little, not quite believing her. "Are you sure? Do you want to sit out the rest of the song?"

"No, I'm fine. Really," she said, trying to emphasize the fact that she was okay.

He still wasn't fully convinced but let the subject drop as the ballad finally ended and gave way to something with a more up-tempo beat.

It was true that Sharon had fun the night before, aside from that little moment when she had allowed herself to dwell on what had happened during lunch. This morning, however, she had allowed herself to think about it all some more. She admitted to herself that she liked Damon. Sure, she thought he was cute and funny, and she acknowledged the fact that so far, he had been genuinely nice to her. She could handle all of that just fine, but his touch… It unnerved her even now in a way she couldn't understand. 'Chill, Sharon. No need to go all crazy here because it probably means nothing.' Still, she couldn't help but think that if there was one thing that could jeopardize her happiness here, it was probably going to be something that involved Damon. Was getting to know him worth the risk?

Sharon's mother patted her daughter on the head a little. "One step at a time, honey," she repeated as she got up to go downstairs. "Just one step at a time."

- - -

Light filtered in through the blinds and fell on the sleeping figure of Damon. He lay sprawled in bed, the covers tangled all about him as he lay on his stomach, his head and arm resting lightly on the pillow. He slept soundly, unaware of anything going on outside the realm of his sleep, until his door was wrenched open and a younger boy and girl came running in. "Wake up, wake up!" a pair of voices screamed.

Damon raised himself up off his bed slightly, very much disoriented. "Huh? What's going on?"

As his brother opened the blinds (causing Damon to shut his eyes in a vain attempt to ignore the bright light), Rosaline took the newly freed pillow from beneath Damon and started hitting her oldest brother with it. "Wake up, wake up, Damon! You promised to take me to the library and read to me!"

Caleb joined in by taking an arm and trying to unsuccessfully pull his brother from the bed when he had collapsed back onto it. "You were going to help me practice at the park, too!"

"Ugh, I didn't say I'd do all that today!" he groaned, hiding his grin by keeping his face turned away from them.

"Yes, you did!" the two whined. "Please?"

"Ros? Caleb? Is your brother up yet?"

"He's awake but we can't get him up out of bed!" Caleb called back to their mom.

"Damon! Get down here and eat some breakfast! I want you to run some errands for me!"

"Okay, mom!" he called back, groaning as he allowed himself to now be successfully pulled out of bed. Not bothering to fix his untidy, black hair or change out of his rumpled T-shirt and shorts, he stumbled down the stairs after his siblings and joined them in the dining room for breakfast. "Good morning," he greeted his mother, kissing her on the cheek and taking the last of the plates from her hands to bring them to the table. "Where's Dad?"

"He's at work," she sighed. "He got volunteered for another project the company's got going on. He should be back for dinner, though."

He nodded as he settled himself into his chair and began helping himself to some food.

"What time did you get home last night, Damon? I didn't hear you come in."

"A little after eleven. The dance ended at ten-thirty but I had to stay behind to help clean up a little."

"But didn't you help set up?"

"Yeah, but it's all right. I just did a couple of things to help."

"All right. Was that new girl there?"

He smiled before he could stop himself. "Yes, Sharon showed up after all."

"That's good. Did she have a good time?"

"I think so. She was laughing when she left."

"Oh, good. Did her parents pick her up?"

"No. Someone drove her home."

"Oh, well that was nice. Anyway, you know what I was thinking? I was thinking that we should take her family out to dinner sometime, make them feel welcome."

"I'll bring it up to her when I see her next week."

Meanwhile, Ros was watching her brother answer their mom's questions. She hadn't missed the smile that had come onto his face at the mention of Sharon and she wrinkled her nose. "Damon, do you like the girl? She might have cooties."

He tried to keep the color from rushing to his face as he answered her, "There are only two women in my life that I like and love, and I know that neither of them has cooties."

"Who are they?"

"You and mom, of course. Now finish your breakfast or we're not going to the library."

Obediently, she turned back to her plate and started eating her breakfast. Damon turned to his left and glared at Caleb, who was giggling. He looked across the table and found his mom sporting a smile. "I don't like her," he stated without being asked and he looked down into his plate to ignore the teasing faces of his family. "Besides, I doubt Dad would approve."

"Your dad means well and wants to make sure you stay focused on your goals," his mom pointed out. "But that doesn't mean we think there's anything wrong with you seeing someone."

"It's only been two days, Mom. I don't know that much about her yet."

"Yet," she repeated after him as she caught the glance of her son, and she smiled. He turned back down to his plate and wished his face would stop burning.

7

Damon listened idly as Ms. Sherwood continued to define and give examples of some math functions to the class. She had been talking for almost thirty minutes straight now and Damon's attention had drifted somewhere in that time. Where his attention drifted had been pretty random. For a moment, he thought about his family, smiling to himself as he remembered how his mother had run out of the house, waving Ros's emergency card and Caleb's lunch just as he had been about to back out of the driveway. He thought about Riley and Vin and the guys for a moment as well and thought about the after school workout they'd be getting in football practice this afternoon. That led him to think about Vin and Mr. West in the room next door and remembered being on the frosh football team with Mr. West as their coach. Damon then thought about a certain girl inside Mr. West's class and tried to fight the sudden urge to smile.

He recounted how he had caught a glimpse of her rushing into the school just as the warning bell had rung. He had watched as she expertly moved her way through the crowds of people moving towards their own respective lockers and classes so she could go to her own locker. He had smiled, said his quick good-byes to the guys, and went to catch up with the girl that had caught his attention in their first literal run-in with each other the week before. "You know, for having only been here for two days, you move through the crowd like a natural," was his greeting to her that morning.

She hadn't bother looking at him when she answered. "Not that hard considering I did this at a high school much larger than this one before."

"Show off," he grinned.

"How do you know I'm showing off? I could just be bluffing and be a real natural, as you call it," she winked to him as she slammed the locker door shut.

"You answered me honestly and without thinking. Now, unless you had that answer rehearsed for a morning just like this so that it would come naturally to you precisely for the moment you may be asked, there'd be no reason for you to be bluffing."

She just laughed at him as they walked quickly up a flight of stairs and on towards their respective classes. "You know, for a Monday morning, you're surprisingly awake. That was a really complicated sentence you just used on me."

"I do that sometimes," he said as they reached her class, grinning. "It throws people off when they realize I'm more than your average, typical jock. Anyway, happy Monday morning," he said, dropping her off.

"You too," she replied before ducking into the classroom.

He himself had taken his seat with just a few seconds to spare, warranting him a look from Ms. Sherwood, a woman who was known to start class promptly after the bell rang.

And now, after almost an hour and a half of calculus, Damon was more than ready for the bell to ring by the time it got around to it. He grimaced slightly to himself as he finished writing down the massive amount of homework Ms. Sherwood assigned to have done by the time Wednesday rolled around and then quickly gathered his things into his backpack. Slinging it onto one shoulder, he made his escape and joined the crowd of people moving in the hallways. Immediately, his eyes scanned the moving faces for familiar ones as he moved slowly along to his next class down in the next wing. Briefly, he caught the sight of Vin dropping Sharon off in one of the other math rooms on this side of the building. In a few strides, Damon had caught up with his friend and the two of them continued onto their English class, but not before he had waved a quick hello to Sharon.

Sharon smiled to herself. It was only her third day at this new high school, and she already felt comfortable with her surroundings. People here had been welcoming, just like she'd mentioned to Vin on Friday, and that surprised her very much. She couldn't believe that there was absolutely no gossip going on behind her back, but it really felt like people were giving her space to reach out when she was ready. Teachers had been more than helpful in making sure that she was up to her peers' level with regards to the work level. Classmates kept asking her if she needed anything and offered their assistance. And without it being said, it had obviously added to her status to have been welcomed into Damon's group so readily.

And that was how she thought of his friends, really. They were Damon's. It wasn't so much the fact that he had been the one to introduce her to the rest of them, but it also hadn't taken her long to realize the influence the boy had over his peers. Just being around him and his friends for two days had shown that to her, how the others seemed to naturally look up to him. And he didn't even really seem to take notice of it. 'The boy's cute, popular, and influential. Just my luck to start liking a guy like him so soon,' she thought to herself.

Sharon shook her head slightly to return herself to the present. She took her seat in the middle of the room towards the back and unzipped her backpack to get her calculus binder out. As she straightened herself up in her seat, however, she found herself staring into a pair of angry blue eyes. Sharon blinked quickly and turned around to see if perhaps she was mistaking herself as the recipient of the girl's animosity for someone else. However, one look told her no one else had sat down behind her yet. Sharon's brow wrinkled a little in confusion as her classmate continued to glower in her direction for a few more seconds before turning away to scribble something furiously onto her paper as the girl in front of the angry girl whispered something to her. Sharon wasn't given a chance to really contemplate this turn of events, however, because more students began filing in and getting settled. The teacher also motioned Sharon up to the front of the class so she could ask her if everything was going all right for her so far. Once Sharon had convinced the teacher that she was doing fine, the bell was about to ring and the girl with the angry blue eyes had been forgotten.

The class came and went, and soon, Sharon found herself packing her things back up into her backpack. As she stood up and started heading towards the door though, she felt a slight tap on her shoulder. Turning, she found the same girl from earlier that morning right behind her, smiling a falsely sweet smile. "Yes?" Sharon asked, feeling her guard starting to come up.

"Let's get one thing straight, all right?" the girl stated point blank as she linked one arm through Sharon's and practically dragged her out of the room and into the hallway, taking full advantage of the noisy crowd to hide out her business with the new girl.

"Excuse me?" Sharon asked, instantly becoming defensive and feeling her guard come up all the way.

"Keep to yourself or with the other losers and leave me to mine." With a dramatic swish of her long blonde hair, she dropped Sharon's arm and turned to go down another hall. "You wouldn't want anything to happen to you now, would you?"

Sharon stayed rooted to her spot, uncertain of what to make of what had just happened. "Cryptic much? And wasn't I just thinking earlier how nice everyone has been so far?" With a final shrug, she realized it was best to let this one go for the time being. 'I suppose there are a few of those types everywhere, and what better target than a new girl? Best to just steer clear of her,' she thought as she turned to race to her next class.

- - -

"So, Sharon…"

The girl glanced to her right and saw Damon looking her way.

"Uh huh?"

"My mom was wondering if you and your family might be up for dinner sometime with us and then maybe show you around."

She smiled. "That's so nice of you and your mom to offer. I'll ask my parents when I get home today and I'll let you know in the morning."

"The morning? Nah. Just call me when you find out," he said as he tore off a corner of his paper and scribbled his phone number on it. As innocent as the act had been and really automatic on his part, he still felt a little heat come to his face when he handed her the scrap and realized how this might look to other people.

Sharon took the slip of paper and placed it in her planner, tactfully ignoring the slightly flushed look on the boy's face. "Thanks, Damon. I'll call you tonight then. You have football practice right after school, right?"

"Up until five, so anytime after that would be all right. You know, though, about my number, please don't hesitate to call if you need something, all right?"

She smiled again and nodded. "Again, thank you."

The two fell into a silent lapse then to work on the drawing assignment Mr. Flynn had given them. A little later though, Sharon voiced a question. "Is this the kind of place where everyone knows everyone else's business?"

"Huh?" Damon replied as he turned in her direction again, curious as to where this question had come from.

She shrugged without taking her eyes off her work. "It's a small town and I get the feeling that everyone seems to know everyone else. I guess I hadn't really anticipated how most everyone would be so nice here."

"I guess so. I never really thought about it, but I guess you're right. Most of us have grown up in this area all our lives."

Another silence fell as Damon continued to think about what she'd said. Then he remembered something. "Most everyone? Has one of the guys been giving you trouble already?" The girl to his left burst out laughing before quickly silencing herself when she saw Mr. Flynn glance in their direction. Damon heard himself grumble a little, although he didn't know whether it was because he didn't like the idea of anyone going after her already or the fact that she was laughing at him. He sincerely hoped it wasn't the latter, although the first thought didn't dwell all that well with him either.

Still smiling, she answered, "I'm sorry. I shouldn't have laughed. No, none of the guys have been giving me trouble."

His brow wrinkled. "A teacher then?"

She shook her head. "Nah, just one of the girls."

"A girl? Why would a girl be acting nasty towards you?"

She shrugged. "I'm wondering the same thing."

"Well, what's her name?"

"I don't know. She never offered it, and I really didn't pay her much attention until this morning."

"What did she say?"

Now, she frowned as she thought back on it but managed to still pull off a shrug. "She said to keep to myself and leave hers alone. I have no idea what she was talking about really."

Damon frowned. "That's weird. Well if you don't know her name, what does she look like? I probably know her if she's in our class and I can talk to her about it."

Again, she shrugged, obviously not caring about the other girl one way or another. "She's a blonde, blue-eyed girl, and she's in my calculus class."

"Well that helps a lot," he scoffed.

"Hey, you asked! Really though, don't worry about it. I don't know what she thinks she knows about me but whatever."

"Well, just let me know if she gives you any more trouble, all right? I meant it earlier about me being willing to help you out, you know."

"I know. After hearing it from your mouth three or four times now, I think I get it," she winked, teasing him.

For some strange reason, Damon found himself blushing again and was grateful Sharon was above mentioning his reaction. 'This girl is really something…'

8

Sharon sat comfortably between her parents in the waiting area of one restaurant. Her mother was on her left, scanning through the menu. Sharon looked to her right and noted that her father was looking a little tired. "Are you okay?"

The man blinked his eyes open and smiled in her direction. "Of course, honey. It was just a long day at work."

She frowned a little. "Still settling in, huh?"

He shrugged slightly. "A little bit, yeah, but it's nothing to worry your mind over," he added. He glanced down at his watch. "Is my watch running a little fast? Mine says it's almost six and we're still here waiting."

"Well, I did tell you that Damon had practice until five. They might be running a little behind." Even as she was saying those words, however, she spotted a hand waving in her direction some distance away. Sharon broke out into a smile and motioned for her parents that Damon and his family had arrived.

"Well they certainly look nice," Sharon's mom said into her daughter's ear before the other family got within hearing range.

"Mom," she smiled. "Would I have even asked if this was okay if I didn't think they would be nice?" Then she turned back towards Damon's approaching family.

"Sharon, it's wonderful being able to put a face to your voice. Mr. and Mrs. Werner, how nice to finally meet you! Welcome to the area! How are you?" Damon's mother immediately embraced each of them in turn, to the surprise of Sharon's family.

"We're doing all right, thank you. And how are you, Mrs. Cardinet?"

"I'm doing wonderful, and please, just call me Maggie. There's no need for formalities here."

"All right, Maggie. I'm Donna, and this is my husband Taylor."

"It's nice to meet you." Next, Maggie turned to her children. "Well, as you may have already guessed, this is Damon. Next to him is Caleb, and the little one is Rosaline," she said, pointing to the little girl in Damon's arms, who shyly peeked at Sharon and her family and smiled a little bit before burying her face back in her older brother's neck.

"Forgive her," Damon said, smiling as he extended a hand to Sharon's parents. "She's a little shy on first encounters, but she'll open up as soon we get her comfortable and fed."

"Yeah. It helps that this is one of her favorite places to eat," Caleb added.

Ros lifted her head just quick enough to stick her tongue out before clutching tightly to her biggest brother again.

"Well then let's sit and eat, shall we? I believe the food is just waiting for us," Maggie announced as she indicated to the hostess they were ready. Within a few moments, they were seated, and a couple minutes of silence descended upon the group as they all looked through the menus for something to eat.

A little bit later, Sharon was still undecided. "What are you getting?" she asked Damon.

He looked up and pointed to an item in her menu. "This. This is the best place to get this dish too so I always have to get it when we come here."

She wrinkled her nose. "It says that it's spicy though."

"Weak," he teased.

"I'd prefer sensitive."

"Well, I can give you a bit to try for yourself. The sauce really isn't that hot."

"Maybe… I guess I'll just go for the broccoli chicken then."

"Good choice," Damon's mom jumped in then. "That's what my husband usually gets when he comes with us."

"Where is he, by the way, if you don't mind my asking," Sharon's mother asked.

"Lawrence actually got stuck at work. He has a couple of big projects he's working on these days and has been pulling overtime every day these past couple of weeks. He really did want to come tonight though and meet with you, but they asked him to stay again."

"Oh, that's all right, Maggie," Sharon's father replied. "I'm sure we can meet up again sometime when it's more convenient."

"Of course. We'll most certainly have to do this again. In the meantime, however, how are you doing? Are you all getting settled in? Do you need anything? Can we help you with anything?"

Sharon's mother smiled, realizing how right Sharon's assessment of the town had been when she'd told her about her first couple of days here. "Well, it's only been about a couple of weeks, yes, but I think we're settling in just fine. As for help though, I have been wondering. Do you know where I can get the best …"

With that, the adults got into a light conversation about the best places to shop or where to go for recreation, stopping only for a little bit to give their orders. Ros and Caleb were preoccupied with a stuffed animal Ros had brought along with her, leaving Damon and Sharon to talk.

"So how was practice today, Damon?"

He shrugged. "Same old, same old. Warmed up, practiced a few drills, played a quick mock game, and then went home to get un-stinky, as Ros would put it," he smiled. "How was your afternoon?"

"Same old, same old. Went home, relaxed for a little bit, got some homework done, and then got ready to come here."

"Well you sure lead a boring life, don't you?"

"It beats getting pushed around and beat up by guys probably more than twice my size."

"Ouch!"

"Literally," she winked.

He groaned. "Ooh, bad joke, Sharon."

"And yet you're smiling. It couldn't have been all that bad, especially if you're one for corny jokes like that."

"Guilty as charged, but only some of the time. And please, don't let anyone else know. That's supposed to be a secret," he winked.

She nodded and tried to keep a straight face. "I will do my best."

Damon turned to his left when he felt a tug on his sleeve. "Yes, Ros?"

"Can you give Doggie a kiss? He's not feeling too well."

"Not feeling too well? Let me see him. Maybe I can find out what's wrong with him."

"No, Damon! He's just sad because Caleb just poked him in the tummy. He wants a kiss."

"All right, a kiss it is then," he said, and he bent down to kiss the stuffed dog on the nose. "All better?"

"All better! Look! He's smiling."

"You're very welcome, Doggie, and wait, what was that?" He brought the dog to his ear and pretended to listen to something it was saying. "Yes, I know Ros is a good mommy for you. She loves you very much."

"No, Damon!" Ros whined. "Doggie doesn't talk! See? His mouth is shut!"

"Forgive me, Ros," he smiled. "I forgot that Doggie doesn't talk, but I could have sworn he said something along those lines to me. Can he whisper?"

"Didn't you hear me? His mouth is shut!"

"All right, all right," he laughed. "I was just imagining things then."

"Duh!"

And with that, Ros turned away from her eldest brother and began playing with Caleb again. Damon, in turn, looked over to Sharon, who was looking right back at him and holding back a laugh.

"What?"

"Duh! Couldn't you see his mouth was shut?"

He tried to come up with a smart remark to throw back at her, but the waiter chose that moment to arrive with their food. He waited until after the waiter had gone before shaking his head and saying, "Just wait, Sharon. I'll get you back for that one."

She looked up at him with innocence plastered on her face. "Get me back for what? I was 'only' pointing out the obvious."

In reply, he just rolled his eyes and turned to his food.

"So, Sharon," Damon's mother started. "What do you think about the high school so far?"

"So far, so good, Mrs. Cardinet. The people have been really nice and welcoming, and the classes aren't too bad. Of course, we're still really early in the semester, so my opinion may change once finals hit, but for right now, I'm liking it."

"That's good to hear. How does it compare with your last high school?"

At this, Damon's ears perked up. He had yet to have brought up anything to do with her past, figuring she'd bring the subject up herself eventually. Sharon's own parents listened for what their daughter had to say, and only they could hear the slight hesitance with which Sharon answered. "Well, this high school's definitely smaller. My last high school was really big. I think we had maybe six or seven hundred students per class? The campus was huge, too as a result. As a freshman, I remembered thinking it would be so easy to stay anonymous because the school was that big and it was harder for me to get to know a lot of the other students or the teachers, but I got used to it. Coming here was a bit of a shock when I realized that the teachers here pretty much know all their students by name."

"No hiding, huh?" Damon asked, teasing and not realizing how Sharon had discussed even that the week prior.

"No hiding," she conceded.

"But you're liking it so far?" Maggie asked.

"Yes, definitely." She turned back to Damon's mom. "It was weird at first because it was so different, but I'm really liking it. It just helps to have people helping me settle in," she added, looking in Damon's direction.

"Good, good. It's nice to know that the high school hasn't changed over the years. It's even better to hear that Damon's being a good boy and minding his manners."

Damon turned to his mom with a look of exasperation on his face. "Mom!" he whined, causing everyone at the table to laugh.

"So, Damon, I hear you're on the football team. Is that right?" Sharon's father questioned, moving the conversation along.

"That's right, Mr. Werner."

"What position do you play?"

"Quarterback, sir."

"Quarterback, huh? I remember when I used to play football in high school…"

"Dad!" It was Sharon's turn to whine, trying to keep him from starting what was sure to be a long-winded story. He paid her no mind, however, and kept on going, finishing that story and then relating a few more over the rest of dinner.

Somewhere in that time, Damon leaned over to Sharon. "Gee, Sharon. I didn't know your dad was quite the talker. I wouldn't have expected someone like him to have helped raise you, considering how quiet you usually are."

She smirked and punched him lightly on the arm in return for the jest. "You have a lot to learn, I see. Just you wait, Damon. There's more to me than you think."

"Oh really? And when will I find that out?"

She shrugged, smiling.

"Uh huh," he chuckled, all the while recognizing the fact that he was becoming evermore intrigued with the girl sitting next to him at the table.

9

"Really, Maggie. You don't have to pay for all our dinners tonight."

"No, no, it's really all right. Tonight is our treat."

"Dinner perhaps, but we're paying for dessert."

"Dessert?" Caleb grinned.

"Of course. Why don't we go for some ice-cream after your mother pays? Wasn't there an ice-cream store just a few doors down?"

"Yes!" Caleb replied before turning to his mother. "Please, please, please can we get some ice-cream?" Ros chimed in as well, and Maggie had no heart to say no.

As Maggie paid for their dinners, the kids made their ways outside. Before she could remind them to not run since it was just after dinner, Caleb immediately bounded ahead and screamed back to everyone to hurry up, impatient for his ice-cream. Ros was as eager as he had been and did her best to keep up with her brother. A shoe caught in a crack in a pavement though, and she tripped, bursting out with tears and crying.

Damon was just exiting the restaurant with Sharon when he saw his little sister seemingly fall in slow motion. Sharon, however, was at Ros's side in a couple of seconds, hugging the girl tight and looking in her purse while the child wailed and hugged a skinned knee to her chest. "Shh, shh. It's okay, Ros. No biggie. See? I've got a band-aid for you right here." She spotted Damon coming at them out of the corner of her eyes and grabbed the stuffed animal from his hand before he could even kneel down to see what was wrong. "And see? Doggie kisses your knee so you can feel better."

Ros's cries quickly downgraded to a whimper as she clutched her dog and peeked at the fresh band-aid on her knee. "Hey! It's my favorite princess! How'd you know?"

Sharon smiled. "Lucky guess," she winked. "Come on now. Up you go. Let's go wash our hands before ice-cream, okay?" With that, she easily picked up the girl in her arms and went straight to the ice-cream parlor a few stores further down, where Caleb had just noticed that something was going on.

"What happened Ros?"

The girl shrugged. "I tripped and fell, but I got a new band-aid. See?" She twisted in Sharon's arms a little to show her brother.

Caleb looked and rolled his eyes. "Ros, you watch that movie every day! Aren't you sick of it yet?"

She answered by sticking out her tongue at him.

"Okay, Ros. Let's get your hands and knee cleaned up a bit before Mom gets here," Damon finally said, reaching for his little sister once they were inside the parlor.

"Okay, but Sharon can take me." She wiggled her way down to the floor and took Sharon by a hand to lead her to the back before she could protest.

"I'm sure Sharon doesn't want-"

"It's fine, Damon," Sharon interrupted him. "I can

take her. Just watch over Caleb and see that nothing else happens in the minute I'm gone and our parents aren't here," she winked, smiling as she followed the girl to the restroom.

When the door closed behind the two girls, a chuckle came from behind the counter. "Always taking orders, aren't you boy?"

Damon grinned to the older man. "I'm not even going to respond to that, Marty. I was just letting the girls bond."

"Seems to me more like she gave you orders to make sure the young'un behaves. Where are your mom and dad, anyway, Damon?"

"Dad's staying overtime at work but Mom should be here in a little bit. She was just paying for our dinner."

As if on cue, Damon's mom and Sharon's parents walked into the parlor just then. "Damon, where are the girls?"

"In the bathroom. Ros tripped and skinned a knee and Sharon's helping her wash up."

"Okay. Do you want to wait on ordering until they get out?"

"No, it's all right. Just go ahead," Donna insisted.

"Okay. Caleb, what do you want?"

"A hot fudge sundae, of course."

"Marty?"

"A hot fudge sundae for Caleb, it is," the old man said with a wink and began his work. "What about you, Maggie dear?" he asked after handing the boy his treat.

"Just a scoop of rocky road, thank you."

"And you, ma'am?" he asked after giving Mrs.

Cardinet her ice-cream.

"My husband and I will just share a scoop of strawberry, if that's all right."

"Perfectly fine," he replied as he turned towards their orders.

"Mommy, mommy! Look at my new band-aid!" a little girl's voice broke in second later.

Maggie laughed when she saw the character bandage. "How fitting. Thank you, Sharon."

"No problem at all, Mrs. Cardinet," she smiled.

"So what does the little princess want today?"

"Hi, Marty! Can I have rocky road with gummi bears on top?"

"Of course."

"And you?" Marty glanced up at Sharon as he prepared Ros's order.

"What about you, Damon? Have you had any yet?"

"Ladies first," Damon and Marty replied together, making Sharon blink a second there.

"All right. Just a scoop of chocolate then, please."

"That's all? After saving the poor princess? I saw you outside the window. Surely you'd want something more of a reward," he teased.

She shrugged. "I'm just a simple girl, I guess."

"All right, all right. Here, have a cherry on top then. My treat," he said, giving Sharon her cup after handing Ros hers.

Sharon grinned. "Thank you."

"Now Damon, my boy. The usual?"

"Of course," he grinned.

A second later, Marty handed him a cone with a scoop of mint chocolate ice-cream. "Thanks."

After a quick debate over who'd pay the bill (Maggie finally gave up trying to convince Sharon's parents that the entire night should have been her treat), they all settled down to enjoy their ice-cream. Ros insisted that she sit in Sharon's lap and the older female was happy to comply. "Are you sure, Sharon? I can take her if you want," Damon said.

"No, it's all right," she replied. "Besides, how can you say no to a little girl's wishes?"

"Easily when the girl is my sister," he grinned.

Sharon rolled her eyes and turned to Ros. "He's such a typical boy, huh Ros? Doesn't he know it's impolite to ignore the wishes of a princess?"

"Nope," the girl giggled.

"Hey! I resent that! And don't be giving her these ideas, Sharon. She's spoiled enough as it is!"

"I highly doubt that. A girl can never be pampered enough. Haven't you learned that by now?"

"I may have heard something like that once or twice before," he conceded. "But really, that just sounds like trouble to me."

"Trouble? What trouble comes from treating little girls extra nice?" she teased.

"Why do I get the feeling that no matter how I answer that question, I'll be wrong?" he grinned.

Sharon grinned back. "Because you're probably right," she confirmed as she had another spoonful of her ice-cream.

"And I would agree with the lady," Marty chose this moment to step in. "Best let her enjoy herself and don't be pestering her or shooing her out of town just yet."

"Whose side are you on, Marty? I've lived here longer than she has!"

"And I've been here even longer, Damon. Trust me - if there's one thing I've learned over the years, it's to never question a woman's word. You'll live longer for it."

"I'll try to keep that in mind," Damon grinned.

"So, anyway, you must be the new folks," Marty said as he stepped out from behind the counter.

"Oh, Marty, yes, of course," Mrs. Cardinet exclaimed. "I'm so sorry I didn't introduce you earlier. This is Mr. And Mrs. Werner and their daughter Sharon."

"It's a pleasure to finally meet you all," he said with a smile.

"Marty here has served the best ice-cream here in town since before I can remember. It certainly beats all those big chain ice-cream brands, and not to mention Marty's one of the nicest people I know."

"Good to know," Sharon's father replied as he and his family said their hellos and settled in to enjoy their dessert and the rest of the evening.

10

A few weeks later, in early October, an announcement interrupted the last period of the day.

"May I have your attention please?" Sharon recognized Ana's voice on the intercom. One look at the clock showed that these announcements were stealing the last five minutes of class, a welcome relief to more than one student that afternoon.

"Sorry for the interruption. As many of you realize, homecoming week is coming up in two weeks. Your student government has been working hard putting everything together but we still need your help. If you would like to participate, please contact a student rep by the end of this week. Also to remind you, homecoming week will be full of rallies and special assemblies. Please refer to the school calendar to see how this affects classes. The game will be that Friday night starting at 7:00 PM. Please show your support for your fellow Dragons and come to the game. Homecoming court will also be announced then, and the dance will be held in the gym the next night, which is Saturday. Doors open at 7:30 and goes on until 11 that night. Make your plans now! You don't want to miss out on any of the fun, trust me. All right, one more announcement and that's that nominations for court will take place next week and voting will occur all during homecoming week. Thanks, and have a great day!"

As the bell rang, announcing the end to another school day, Sharon put away her notebook and pen in her backpack before joining everyone in exiting the room. She fought against the crowd and made her way back up the stairs to go to her locker to get the rest of her things. Before she made it though, she saw a friendly face waiting for her. "Hey, Sharon."

"Vin! What's up?" she smiled.

He raised a hand and rubbed the back of his neck shyly. "Nothing much. I just wanted to ask you something."

"Really? Well ask away," she said as she opened her locker door.

"I was just wondering if you were going to the homecoming dance."

"Oh, I don't know. Maybe. I haven't really thought about it yet but I guess I should, huh, seeing as it is only a couple weeks away."

"Well, uhh… Do you want to go with me?"

Sharon gave a warm smile. "There goes having to think about who to ask. Thanks, Vin. Sure, I'd be happy to go with you."

The nervous look on his face disappeared to be replaced with one of relief. "Great! Here, let me get that for you," he offered, taking a couple of books from her hand and tucking them under one arm.

"Vin!" she laughed. "You don't have to do that."

"It's all right. I'll walk you to your car. I've got some time before practice starts."

She shook her head, smiling. "If you insist…"

"I do," he grinned back at her. "Besides, I need to

work out details with you."

"Details? What kind of details are you looking for?"

"Oh you know, the usual. There's the dinner, the ride, your dress color…"

"Whoa, whoa, whoa," Sharon laughed. "Aren't you getting ahead of yourself? I don't even have a dress yet! I wasn't kidding when I said I'd hardly given homecoming much thought."

Vin blushed. "Sorry. It's just that it's two weeks away already and I feel like I've been procrastinating."

"Two weeks is plenty of time, Vin. What's to worry?"

He shrugged. "Most of the girls here started thinking about homecoming when school started. For some reason, I just assumed you did too."

She chuckled. "I guess I should have realized that something like this would be a big deal here."

"It ranks up there with winter vacation and the spring festival."

"Ahh, I see," she nodded. "Well then, I guess we have a bit of planning to do."

Vin agreed. "But we can definitely talk about this later. Thanks for agreeing to go to the dance with me, Sharon," he said before giving her a quick hug once they reached her car.

"You're very welcome," she replied before he turned to jog off to practice. 'Homecoming dance, huh? Wait until Kelly hears about this,' she thought to herself as she drove home.

- - -

"You look happy today, Vin. What's up?" Riley asked as he changed into his practice jersey in the gym locker room.

"I just asked Sharon to the dance," he grinned.

"And I'm assuming she said yes by the look on your face. Congrats," Vin's teammate patted him on the back. "I told you it wasn't going to be a big deal."

"Easy for you to say. I bet you and Ana don't even ask each other to dances anymore since it's assumed."

"Of course I have to. It makes me look good," he winked.

"Riley looking good? When does that ever happen?"

"Very funny, Damon," Riley answered. "You're late."

"Not late. Just later than usual. I had to talk to Plopper. What were you guys talking about?"

"Vin here has just gotten himself a date to the dance," Riley pointed to where Vin was changing into his practice gear a couple lockers down.

"Congrats, Vin. Who's the lucky girl?"

"Sharon," he grinned back.

Lucky for Damon, no one noticed the surprised look on his face. All faces had turned towards Vin, who blushed lightly from the attention. As their fellow teammates congratulated him, Damon knew he was sincerely happy for his friend, that Vin, the undeclared shyest one of the group, had finally gotten the courage to ask someone to the dance. 'But Sharon? I was going to ask her. Great…'

He turned to open his locker and stuff his

backpack into the bottom of it. 'Then again, it's not like I was making it obvious I was going to do that or anything,' he continued to think. 'We don't hang out much outside school because I've got practice and games, and when we do hang out, it's with the gang. At school, the most we ever get a chance to talk is during lunch or art class. No, Damon, you never had a claim on her. Vin had as much right to ask her as you did.'

However, he had to wonder if that last thought was really enough to make him feel any better about the situation and sighed. He thought back to the first couple of days of school and the attraction he'd felt for her then and even up to now. 'And I've been too scared to do anything about it all this time…'

The shutting of a locker door snapped him out of his thoughts. 'All right, so the topic will just have to be put on hold again,' he mused as he grabbed his helmet out of the locker and shut the door with a slam. 'Tonight, Damon. You're thinking about this tonight after practice,' he promised himself.

Riley met Damon at the locker room door. "You okay, D? You got a little quiet there."

"I'm all right. Just thinking about who to take to homecoming is all. I totally forgot about it until the announcement."

"Forget about homecoming? You're on board! How can you forget about it?"

"I didn't say I forgot about homecoming, goof. Just forgot about asking someone."

Riley grinned. "Well that shouldn't be too hard to think about. There are plenty of girls who wouldn't mind going out with the star of the school that night," he winked.

"True, but it's our last homecoming. Ever thought about that? It has to be with someone special, you know?"

"I swear, Damon. You think like a girl too much sometimes. This is our senior year! Don't think too hard."

"I guess…"

"Damon! Riley! No more talking. Get over here and start stretching!" their coach barked at them.

With that, Damon shook his head of all homecoming thoughts and focused on the practice.

- - -

"Guess what."

"What?"

"Guess!"

"Sharon, just tell me already!"

"I'm going to the homecoming dance!"

"That's great! I told you Damon would ask you out sooner or later."

"…"

"Sharon?"

Sharon balanced the phone on her shoulder as she opened her closet. "Damon didn't ask me to the dance, Kelly. Vin did."

"Oh. But I thought you liked Damon."

Sharon didn't disagree. "I do like Damon, but it's not like I could say no to Vin. He's a nice guy too."

"You don't like him though, do you?"

"No, I don't. He's just a friend and I have him in my government class. Come on, Kelly. Be happy for me. I'm going to my first real dance here."

"I am happy for you, Sharon, but I'm just wondering why in the world you didn't ask Damon earlier!"

"Because I was only reminded this afternoon that the dance was two weeks away and Vin literally asked me to go with him two minutes after the announcement was made."

"Excuses, excuses. You better be going to the winter dance with Damon then or else!"

"Or else what?"

"Or else I'll go down there and ask him for you myself!"

"Kelly!" Sharon laughed. "You haven't even met the guy! I don't think he'd appreciate a complete stranger giving him orders like that."

"Well it's either I do exactly that or you ask him by the time Thanksgiving break comes around."

"We'll see about that. Things may change."

"Highly unlikely. I know you. Once you're stuck on a guy, you're stuck good… Well, at least until a certain James is free," Kelly laughed.

"I'm going to pretend I didn't hear that."

"Do you want me to repeat it for you?" came the cheeky response.

"That's really all right, thanks," Sharon chuckled.

"So anyway, what are you going to wear to this homecoming dance?"

"Oh, I don't know. I'm actually looking in my closet right now to see if any of my old dresses will work."

"What's the fun in that? You should go out and get something new."

"I would, but money's getting a little tight since I wasn't able to work this summer and I haven't exactly been looking for a job, though I probably should now that I have a better sense of my days here. I really should start looking for something…"

"Well, let me know if you need anything, Sharon. I've gotta get going and help my mom set the table. We're about to have dinner. I'll talk to you later?"

"Definitely. Bye, Kelly."

"Bye."

Sharon clicked the phone off without taking her eyes away from her closet. 'Hmm… Now, which dress should I wear…'

11

"Oh my gosh, Sharon. Come in, come in. Thank goodness you're here. I really am so sorry this is all such short notice-"

"No problem, Mrs. Cardinet. Anything to help out. You've been so nice to me and my family, it's the least I could do."

"You're such a sweetheart, thank you. Anyway, let me get the kids." Damon's mother turned towards the staircase. "Caleb! Ros! Come downstairs please. Sharon's here!"

A squeal preceded the pounding of footsteps coming down the stairs. "Sharon!" Ros screamed as she ran to the other girl with outstretched arms.

"Hello, Ros," Sharon answered as she swung the little girl into her arms for a hug. "How's the princess doing today?"

"Good. Do you want to play dolls with me?"

"Maybe in a minute. Let me just show Sharon where everything is first, okay Ros?" Maggie suggested.

Ros agreed and hopped down from Sharon's arms. Sharon gave Caleb a quick hello when she passed him upon following Mrs. Cardinet to the kitchen.

"Now the numbers are all posted here on the board behind the phone in case you need anyone. My husband will be at work, I'll be here at the hall for a meeting," she pointed to one number. "And Damon's cell phone number is here in case you can't get a hold of anyone else. Here's their doctor's number as well and the other emergency numbers." She turned back to Sharon. "Now the kids just got in a few minutes before you and I already gave them a snack, so they should be fine until dinner. If they get a little hungry though, there are some crackers in the cupboard. Ros can show those to you. What else…"

Sharon smiled. "I think I've got it, Mrs. Cardinet. You told me everything else last night, and if I really do need anything else, I'll just call. Besides, it's not like I haven't babysat before."

"I know, I know, and thank you too for your referrals last night. I appreciate that. Mothers will always worry though, and you know that too," she replied. Then she turned to her kids. "Okay, you two. I'm going to get going now. Be good while I'm gone, all right? Your father and your brother will be here in a few hours and I'll see you a little later tonight, all right?"

Sharon watched from nearby as Mrs. Cardinet kissed the two children on their foreheads while hugging them tight and then rushing out the door with purse and keys in hand. "Come on, you two," Sharon said as she led the way back into the living room. "Now that it's just the three of us, tell me what you usually do at this time."

"Well, our other sitter usually lets us play in the backyard," Caleb replied, smiling hopefully.

"I had a funny feeling you'd say that, but what I was actually thinking was that we should get least get some of your homework done first." As expected, Damon's siblings groaned at the concept. Sharon chuckled. "I think your parents would be happier if you at least started it. I'll tell you what though. You guys get all your homework and bring it in here. I can help you both out for half an hour or so and then we can maybe play in the backyard or even the park. How does that sound?"

"But I want to play now," Ros whined.

"In a little while, princess. Now go get your things. The more you get done now, the sooner we can go play. We could even start a movie later if you finish it all. We could have popcorn and everything."

"Promise?" Caleb asked.

"I promise," Sharon replied.

That was enough incentive for both to go charging back up the stairs to get their things.

Two hours later, shrieks and laughter were coming from the backyard as the three of them played their own version of hot potato. The afternoon sun was just beginning to dip lazily from the sky. Sharon was tossing the soft ball between her two hands, pretending it was hot, before calling to Caleb. "Here, Caleb. Catch!" She threw the ball in his direction. As Caleb and Ros continued to throw the ball to each other, Sharon announced that she was going inside to get some punch for them. She slipped inside and walked over to the counter to get the three juice boxes Ros had taken out, keeping an eye on the younger two at all times.

Sharon stepped back out onto the back porch, sliding the glass door behind her shut. She sat herself down on a step and helped herself to one of the juice boxes while she watched Ros chase Caleb around the backyard. Sharon looked down at her watch and noticed that it was nearing 5:30. 'Ahh, I'll just let them play until someone gets home. There's no point in having them come in now to go back to their homework only to be distracted again as soon as someone comes home,' she thought. 'Besides, those two actually worked hard for two hours.'

Sure enough, the sound of the garage door opening came only a few minutes later. If it had been possible – Sharon couldn't tell herself – the shrieking from the backyard increased as the two kids raced back towards the house. Sharon tossed Ros and Caleb their juice boxes as they raced by her before following them in herself.

"Daddy!" Ros shrieked, arms stretched out. "You're home early!"

"I am. I missed you so much, I just had to go," he said as he stooped down to give Ros a hug and a kiss on the cheek.

"Does that mean you have to stay later tomorrow?" Caleb panted slightly, frowning a little.

"Maybe, Caleb, but probably not," the father answered, giving him a hug as well. "This case is finally coming to an end, meaning I can actually come home and torment you all again," he smiled.

As Mr. Cardinet stood up, his eyes finally rested on Sharon, who had stood back from the small family reunion. "Hello, Mr. Cardinet," she greeted, finally stepping up and extending a hand.

"Hello…"

"Sharon," she supplied.

"Ahh, Sharon. It's a pleasure to finally meet you," he smiled as he shook her offered hand. "The mom got you to babysit today, I'm guessing?"

Sharon nodded. "That's why I'm here."

"Board meeting?" Again, she didn't disagree with him. "That means it's my turn to cook then, I see. All right, let's move to the kitchen. Kids, go wash up. You're helping me cook tonight."

As the children rushed to do as their father had said, Mr. Cardinet turned to Sharon. "Thanks a lot for looking over the kids today."

"You're welcome, Mr. Cardinet. To be honest, it was fun. These two are really nice, well-behaved kids."

"And Damon's not?" he grinned.

"Damon's not a kid," she grinned back.

"Ahh, too true. It seems we're all growing up faster these days. Well then, I guess it's best for you to get on home now. Here's what we owe for your time here today," he said as he paid Sharon. "Thank you again for helping us out."

"And again, you're very welcome," she replied with a firm handshake.

"Are you going away now?"

Sharon turned to where Ros was standing at the foot of the staircase.

"Uh huh. Your daddy's here now so I don't have to watch you anymore."

"Will you be back tomorrow?"

Sharon smiled. "I'll be back if your parents want me to come back, okay?"

"Okay," the little girl nodded.

Sharon reached down to give the girl one last

hug good-bye. "Bye, Caleb," she called towards the kitchen where the boy was already getting stuff out for dinner. She gathered her backpack and with a final farewell, she was out the door.

The sun had still not quite set by the time she reached her car. She opened the passenger side to place her backpack on the seat before going to the driver's side. She had just turned on the ignition when another car pulled up into the Cardinet driveway. With a grin, she waved to Damon as he jumped out of his car to see who it was.

When he realized it was Sharon, he waved for her to hold on. She stopped the car and rolled down her window. "What's up, Damon?"

"Just wanted to say hi. What are you doing over here?" he asked, coming to lean by her window.

"Your parents needed an emergency sitter and I guess your mom overheard us talking about it one time. She called me last night to ask. Didn't you know?"

He shook his head. "I had no clue. I thought our normal sitter would be here."

She shrugged. "I don't know. I just came because your mom asked me to."

"So why are you leaving?"

"Your dad's home. You should go in and say hi."

"Trying to get rid of me now, huh?"

Sharon rolled her eyes but smiled, nonetheless. "As much as I really do enjoy your company, I've got to get home. I've got a lot of homework to get started on, and I'm sure you do too."

Damon grinned and eased himself away from the window. "All right. I see how it is. Your homework is more important than me," he said with an overly dramatic sigh.

"Damon!" she laughed. "You're not making this any easier for me to go."

"And why should I be making things easier? You're the one who wants to leave."

'Who said anything about that?' she wondered to herself. "Look, I'll see you tomorrow, okay?"

"Fine, but you're going to make up for not staying longer tonight."

"Oh? And how am I going to do that?"

"Come early to school tomorrow. Go to the student center, and be there by 7:15. The door closest to the school will be unlocked."

"7:15!" she screeched. "That's a full forty-five minutes before school starts! What the heck am I going to do with all that time?" she demanded.

Damon, however, had already jogged back to his car to get his things from the trunk. With another wave and smile, he turned towards his house.

Seeing as she wasn't going to get an answer from him, Sharon turned the ignition to her car and closed the window, all the while shaking her head. "You just had to pick him huh, Sharon?" she muttered to herself as she finally pulled away from the curb, waving good-bye to Damon as he watched her drive off before he finally stepped inside.

12

The sound of the alarm clock woke Damon from his sleep. He rolled over onto his stomach and placed his pillow over his ears to try and block out the sound. After a minute of that unsuccessful attempt to muffle the annoying, incessant beeping, he emerged from under his blanket and slammed a hand down on the off button. He lay back on his bed and draped one arm over his eyes. "Just a few more minutes…"

A knock came on the door.

"Damon, honey, you're going to be late," his mother said through the door.

He groaned and finally rolled himself out of bed. "6:00… Who in their right minds gets up this early?" he asked himself as he padded off to his bathroom. He blinked hard when he flipped the light switch on and then looked in the mirror. "Man, oh man, D. You sure look terrible." He shook his head and turned on the faucet. He splashed the cold water onto his face and instantly, he was awake. "That's better," he muttered. "No more droopy eyes. Now let's see if we can't tidy up the rest of you."

Ten minutes later, Damon was done with the bathroom and was rummaging through his closet for something decent to wear. He grabbed a pair of khaki pants and shrugged those on. Next, he took a black dress shirt from one hanger and put that on. He looped a red tie around his neck, stuffed his feet into a pair of black shoes, and grabbed his letter jacket and backpack before heading down the stairs.

"It's about time," his mother greeted him with a kiss on one cheek. "But at least you look good. Do you plan on breaking any hearts today?" she teased.

"Thanks for the support, mom. You know it's tradition for the team to dress nicely homecoming week."

"I know, I know. I'm just kidding. Anyway, the donuts are by the door. Don't forget them on the way out, okay?"

"You're the best, mom," he said as he finished tying his shoes. He slipped on his jacket and backpack and headed towards the front door. "Thanks for taking Ros and Caleb to school today, too."

"Tradition is tradition. Just go to school and have breakfast already."

"Will do. I love you, mom."

"I love you, too. See you tonight."

"Bye!"

And with that, Damon scooped up the three boxes of donuts from the small stand beside the door and walked out to greet the sun.

- - -

6:45 came and it was Sharon's alarm clock that rang now. She woke up easily, turning over to her right and switching the alarm to off before stretching her body and giving a big yawn. Then she threw off her covers and left her bedroom to go to the bathroom. Once done in there, she went back to her room and changed out of her flannel pajamas into a pair of jeans, a white, long-sleeved T-shirt, and a red, hooded flannel vest over that. She brushed her hair and decided to let it stay loose for once instead of tying it back like she normally did.

The clock read 7:01 and she sprinted out of her room, keys and backpack in hand and into the kitchen. She grabbed an apple off the table for her breakfast and raced out the door.

She reached the student center at 7:14.

- - -

"Sharon! You made it just in time! And look at you! Your hair is down for once!" Damon greeted. "Here's an apron." He threw her an extra one.

"Thanks for the good morning. What the heck am I supposed to do with this?"

"You just volunteered yourself to helping serve breakfast this morning," he grinned.

"I did 'what'? I so did not volunteer myself. You did!"

"You came, didn't you?"

She scowled at him but gave in and put on the apron after placing her backpack among the pile already there.

"Sharon! What are you doing here?"

She turned her head and smiled. "Hey, Ana. Damon tricked me into volunteering today. I even missed making myself breakfast and lunch to make sure I came on time."

"He did, did he?" Ana turned to give Damon an evil eye.

He raised his hands up in defense. "Sorry. How was I to know? Now I feel bad. Here, why don't you just get a plate and some food and eat. You don't have to help," he offered.

"No, it's all right. I'm here to help so that's what I'll do. Just save me a chocolate donut for breakfast, okay Damon? Now Ana, what do you want me to do?"

"Are you sure you don't want to eat yet?"

"Half an hour is nothing. I'll be fine."

"Okay. Then just go over there and stand in between Riley and Vin. You can help with the cereal."

"Ooh, fun stuff," she winked and made her way over to where the two guys were. "Good morning," she greeted them.

"Sharon! Hi," Vin smiled, reaching over to give her a hug. Riley nodded and smiled a hello and then turned back to a conversation he was having with another football player to his right. "What are you doing here?" he asked as he poured one student some cereal into a cup.

"Ana says cereal duty."

He laughed. "No, I mean what are you really doing here? Why are you helping the varsity football team and student government feed the freshmen and the faculty this morning?"

"Ask Damon that one. He's making me do this."

"Is he really? Well, he does have a way of getting people to do what he asks."

"He and Ana both, huh?"

He nodded. "There's a reason why they're in charge of student government. You couldn't ask for a more dedicated and hard-working pair. Those two, they work wonders together. It makes sense and all, what with them knowing each other since they were practically born and knowing how to always do what it takes to get the results they want."

Sharon looked over to where Damon was standing with one arm draped over Ana's shoulders. The two were talking with one of the teachers, all smiling and laughing away. 'Together, huh,' she thought. 'You really do know the right guys to pick, Sharon. Looks like you're out of luck in this department if they're a couple. I always see them together so it makes sense. Oh well.'

"Sharon?"

She forced herself to look away and focus back on the present. "Huh?"

"I just asked you if you knew what color your dress was yet and you kinda just blanked on me."

"Sorry, Vin," she smiled sheepishly. "You know… Cereal… It's so fascinating sometimes…"

He gave her an odd look.

"All right. That wasn't the most brilliant response ever, was it?"

"You can say that again," he grinned. "What was on your mind?"

"Oh, nothing really. But before I forget to answer your question again, I'm going to be wearing a black dress."

"All black?"

She shook her head. "It has a sparkly silver floral

pattern."

"Okay, simple enough. Have you thought about where you would maybe like to eat?"

"Dinner too? Vin, that's a lot of money!"

"Come on, it's homecoming. Besides, it's not like you're going to be paying."

"What do you mean? Of course I am. I can't let you do that."

"Yes, you can. It'll be my treat. Consider it a belated welcome to our humble high school from me."

"No, really, you don't have to do that. I feel bad now."

"Don't. Just think about it, okay? We could even do a trip to McD's if you feel bad about the money. I just think we should have dinner beforehand."

She shook her head but smiled. "You really want to go all out for this, don't you?"

"It's senior year, Sharon. We gotta make it memorable."

"You do have a point," she conceded. "I'll think about it then."

"You do that, and here, have some cereal. You look like you're hungry."

"A little bit," she admitted. "Was it that obvious?"

"Your witty comment about cereal and your stomach growling made it so," he winked.

"Again, blame Damon for that one. In order to get here on time, I had to skip breakfast at home and I didn't have time to make my lunch either."

"Well then, I say you've done your duty here. Go ahead and eat up. Breakfast is pretty much wrapping up anyway. There's plenty more cereal if you want though. And after you finish with that, we can go to our lockers and then off to government."

She chuckled, agreeing and thanking him before taking one cup of cornflakes and sitting herself down in a nearby chair to eat.

13

"Has anyone told you how lovely you look tonight?"

Sharon turned around and inwardly caught her breath, fully approving of the sight before her. Her face eased into a smile. "Thanks, Damon. You don't look too shabby yourself, you know. And before I forget, good game yesterday," she added, hugging him warmly.

"Thanks," he smiled before looking down at himself. "I do look pretty good tonight, don't I?"

She laughed. "Ever the modest one."

"I try," he smiled back easily. "Anyway, did you just get here?"

She nodded her head. "Just a few minutes ago. You?"

"I'm on board, remember? I've been here since an hour before the dance started."

"So dedicated of you."

"Just doing my duty. Besides, it's supposed to get me out of clean up duty afterwards," he smiled. "So, would you like to dance?"

"With you?"

He rolled his eyes. "Of course with me. I'm the one asking."

"But don't you have a date?"

"I do, but she's not here yet. Besides, I don't see Vin around anywhere."

She shrugged. "I lost him as soon as we got in when I went to drop my coat off at the front table."

Damon accepted her answer with a nod and a smile. "So are we going to dance or just keep talking then?"

"Well, since you asked so nicely, I guess we can keep on talking..." she teased.

He rolled his eyes and grabbed her hand anyway, pulling her towards the dance floor. "Come here, you."

Sharon laughed as he led them to the slowly growing crowd on the dance floor, leading them right into the middle of the pack. The two found themselves moving easily to the fast beat with each other. As one song flowed into another, and then the next, the rest of the world melted away, leaving her with just him and music. She smiled. 'I could get used to this,' she let herself think for a moment. 'What am I thinking? I'm here with Vin! Where is he anyway?' she wondered.

As if in answer to her thoughts, Sharon felt a hand rest lightly on her shoulder. "Vin!" she smiled when she saw him behind her. Immediately, the rest of the world came back to her.

"Hey, Sharon," he smiled, nodding to Damon before taking Sharon's hands in his and leading her away just a little bit.

She turned around to say bye to Damon in time to see a hand catch Damon's arm. She heard a sickly sweet voice say his name, and then suddenly, too many people separated Damon and Sharon, Vin having drawn her too far away to let her identify the girl. She shrugged it off for the moment, turning back to Vin. "Sorry about that," he was saying as the two started to dance together. "One of the guys wanted my opinion on something."

"Oh, don't worry. I understand."

He smiled again, and the two continued to dance for a while yet, Sharon laughing and smiling easily with her friend.

A few more minutes passed and Vin's arms gently encircled Sharon's waist as they danced to the first slow song of the night.

"So have you thought about where you want to go to college?" Sharon was asking as they danced.

"Yeah. I know I'm definitely going to be moving to the west coast."

"Oh?"

"Yeah. I feel the need for a change of scenery really. I've got some family over in California too, so it wouldn't be like I'm all alone either. I have an uncle down around LA and my older brother's in San Francisco. I have the applications for the UC system there and I should have those done and sent out in a few more days."

"That's great," Sharon smiled. "Where's your top choice?"

"Honestly, it's-"

She listened intently as Vin talked about where he wanted to go, smiling at the enthusiasm he presented at the idea of college. As the two danced slowly, Sharon's eyes fell on Riley, who was dancing on the other side of the floor with Ana. Confusion set in for Sharon when she noticed how close the two were – neither was talking, their eyes were both closed, and really, it seemed they were just standing in time, not dancing at all. 'Is she okay? I thought she was with-'

Sharon's eyes found Damon off the dance floor and at one of the tables. He'd taken a break from dancing and was laughing with a few of his other friends. 'I'm so confused... I thought Ana and Damon are a couple...' She shrugged her thoughts off for the moment though as the slow song ended and a faster beat started to play.

"Hey," Vin said. "I think the gang's all here. We should probably take pictures now before the line gets too long."

Sharon nodded. "Sounds like a plan."

Vin started to lead the way to Riley, but got stopped along the way by a couple of his friends just to say hi. By the time they got to Riley, they found him talking to a fellow teammate, and Ana was nowhere in sight.

"Hey, aren't we supposed to be doing pictures soon?" Vin asked.

Riley nodded. "But I guess student government are getting done first, so that's where Ana and Damon are now."

"Well, we may as well round the rest of the gang up and wait in line so that they don't have to wait too long when they're done."

Riley nodded and they all left the dance floor to get the rest of the group.

The task proved to be easier said than done though. While it was certain that everyone arrived, everyone was just so spread out, it took a full twenty minutes to gather everyone together. People had still been out on the dance floor, while a couple of the other couples had already gotten in line to get their pictures done... Eventually though, twenty people had been gathered and were left deciding on how to pose.

"Guys on one side and girls on the other with our beloved Homecoming King and Queen in the middle?" Riley suggested.

"No way! Couples have to stay together!" Sharon heard one of the girls say.

"Well then, how are we going to do this?"

"How about yeah, letting the Homecoming couple stay in the middle, but with their own dates?"

The idea was accepted, and Sharon watched as Ana and Damon stood back to back in the center, Ana's arms around Riley and Damon's hands around another girl...

Sharon grimaced. It was the girl that had been rude to her from her calculus class. Before she could think anything else of it, she let the photographer lead her over to the center of the picture as well, where Vin knelt down on one leg in front of Ana and motioned for Sharon to sit on his other leg. She obliged and one of the other couples mirrored them in front of Damon and his date.

"Hey Sharon! Hi Vin," Ana said, bending down to give them an awkward hug while everyone else figured out the rest of the pose. "It's good to see you here!"

"Same to you," Sharon replied. "I can't believe I'm only saying hi to you now."

"Oh, I know! I'm so sorry, but you know, duties beckon, and I must obey. Hopefully now though, everything's done and I can actually enjoy the rest of the dance with you guys."

"You better," Vin smiled. "Otherwise, I know Riley's going to be mighty upset with you."

For once, the football player just stayed silent, shrugging and wrapping his arms back around Ana in a close embrace as they all got ready for their first pose. The photographer handed Ana and Damon their crowns and then quickly returned to his position behind the camera.

A couple shots later, it was all done. As Sharon and Vin got up, she felt another hand on her shoulder. It was Damon. "Kari," he was saying. "You know Vin. Have I introduced you yet to Sharon?"

Sharon turned her attention to the blonde next to him and did her best to not let the smile on her face drop as she extended a hand. "It's nice to meet you, Kari," she said.

The blonde took the hand for the briefest second and barely glanced her way. "Vin, you did great in the game yesterday. You know, the team next year is going to be really hurt what with you, Riley, and Damon all leaving."

Sharon forced herself to not roll her eyes at the snub she'd been given by one of the school's top cheerleaders as Kari continued to praise the guys. 'I wonder if the guys know about her attitude off the field,' she thought as Riley and Ana led the way back out onto the dance floor.

– – –

Her hair was down for the night, but instead of the normal straight and sleek look, she had added some large curls to just give her hair some extra volume. Again, she left her face simple, only adding a touch of eyeshadow and some lip gloss to her otherwise plain face. Simple, diamond teardrop earrings hung from her ears, and a matching necklace encircled her neck. Her sleeveless dress was black, and it ended a couple of inches above her knee. A slight silver pattern of flowers shone off the dress, depending on how the light hit it. Black heels, a wide smile, and the sparkle in her eyes finished off the ensemble.

Damon found himself looking at Sharon, watching as she danced in Vin's arms. It was another slow song, and he found himself with his own arms wrapped ever so lightly around Kari. His mind, however, was not on the blonde right in front of him. He was thinking about earlier that night, from the time he had led Sharon onto the dance floor by the hand and to the time Vin and Kari had interrupted their dancing...

There was no denying it. They had moved well together. Now, what that meant to him, he had no clue. 'She's definitely a nice girl,' he thought to himself. 'So genuine, unlike other girls.' He looked down at Kari and knew she was a prime example of the kind of girl he didn't want to end up with in the future. Where Kari was all talk and looks and shallow ambition, Sharon had so far been all heart and depth – he knew more about Sharon than he did Kari, and Kari's family had moved into the area when they were still in elementary school and so had grown up in the same area. 'Like that means anything,' he thought to himself. 'We were just never close. Sharon though... She's something else...'

As if she knew that he'd been thinking about her, Sharon looked up at just that moment and found herself looking straight into Damon's eyes. She blinked in surprise and then smiled, matching the one Damon sent her way before she turned her attention back to whatever Vin and she were talking about.

'Yup, she's definitely something else,' he thought as the dance ended and the night continued on.

14

"Sharon! Phone!"

"Thanks, Mom!" she yelled back from her room. She rolled over on her bed and quickly grabbed the phone. "Hello?"

"Sharon!"

"Hey Kelly! Long time, no talk. What's the news?" Sharon beamed when she heard her best friend on the other end.

"No way! I called to find out how your dance was last night."

Sharon laughed. "I thought you were going to wait until I sent you pictures!"

"Yeah right! I want to know right now, what you ended up wearing, were you able to do anything after the dance, if there was any more eye candy for you or were your eyes glued on a certain quarterback all night. I want the news!"

Sharon laughed again but answered, "I wore my homecoming dress from last year like I thought I would because I had no time or money to get anything else, no, we didn't do anything after the dance, Vin just drove me home afterward because you know how my parents can be about curfew now, and no, my eyes were not glued on Damon all night, I was there with Vin!"

"Uh huh, but just because you were there with someone else, which I still don't know why you didn't ask Damon yourself in the first place what with this crush thing going on, doesn't mean you're always focused on what's right in front of you."

"Kelly, stop it," she laughed. "You know I didn't ask him because Vin asked me first, and not to mention there was the fact that I thought he was going out with Ana, but still, you're right. My mind did wander off a couple of times, only I ended up thinking about you and everyone else back home and missing you guys terribly."

"Oh how sweet, but you're such a liar!" Kelly laughed. "I bet you didn't think of us at all last night. That's why I'm calling you first thing on a Sunday morning because 'someone' didn't call me first."

"Oh please, it's barely eleven o'clock. I'm surprised you're even up at this hour!"

"Don't even try changing the subject, Sharon. You're not going to get away with it! I want to know what happened last night down to the last detail!"

Sharon laughed. "Nothing changes with you, Kelly. All right, all right. So Vin got here about 6:00 yesterday looking really good. He was wearing a nice suit that he'd gotten for one of his cousins' weddings earlier this year."

"Well if that was the case," Kelly interjected. "Then of course he'd look good. I don't know of a guy yet who doesn't look at least ten times better dressed up!"

"Very true. Anyway, so of course, he gives me my corsage, three red roses bunched together, all pretty of course and you know how I can't describe this kind of stuff so bear with me, and I gave him his boutonniere. Of course, there are pictures for the next ten, fifteen minutes or so and my parents are all fussy and stuff. Then we leave for dinner downtown. Talk was pleasant, we were just talking of our families and classes and the workload and such. Then we got to the dance a little after 7:30. One of his friends pulled him aside while we were putting our stuff down. Damon found me and took me out to the floor to dance-." Sharon paused for a moment to let Kelly finish her shriek before continuing. "Before Vin came back. We danced to a couple songs, the DJ, by the way, was decent, and then we took pictures. Apparently, Ana went to the dance with Riley and Damon went with that girl with the attitude from my calculus class, her name's Kari. She totally snubbed me when Damon was formally introducing us but oh well. We all went back out onto the dance floor and danced or hung out at our table, the dance ended at 11:00 and we hung out for a couple, making the excuse that we were waiting for Ana and Damon to finish overseeing the beginnings of clean-up before we all split to go our separate ways. As I said, I have pictures from all throughout the night, and I'll send those to you as soon as I can get them up but that's pretty much it. Vin dropped me off last night about 11:30, 11:45, we said our good nights, and I went to bed. Done."

There was a slight pause on the other end, and Sharon waited patiently for whatever was coming next. "You danced with Damon!!"

"Yes, and Vin and Riley and a couple of the other

guys too, but mostly Vin."

"Sharon!!"

"Kelly!" she answered back, laughing.

"Must I force all these answers out from you?" she practically groaned. "Well, is he a good dancer? What'd you guys talk about? Is there something going on between you two?"

"Yes, nothing really, we just danced, and I don't think so," she answered quickly.

"Sharon, you're impossible!"

"And that's why I'm going to be single for the holidays, right?" she laughed.

"Oh please, let's not go there again. You don't know that. Besides, what's this talk about Ana and Damon not being together? Have you asked him yet?"

"Of course not! That's not my business!"

"Hello? You guys are at least friends. That's a fair question."

"Mm, maybe. If anything else, I'll ask Ana about it later," she replied.

Again, Kelly sighed. "You're never going to go out with Damon at that rate, Sharon!"

Sharon just laughed back. "We'll see, Kelly. If it's meant to be, it's meant to be. If not, then who am I to ruin a good friendship in the meantime?"

"And possibly miss out on something great in your life?"

"We'll see," she repeated once more.

- - -

Mr. Cardinet looked up from his newspaper as

Damon walked into the kitchen, still half-asleep. "Did you have a good time last night, Damon?"

"Good morning, Dad. Yeah, I had a good time."

"And your date, what's her name. Did she have a good time?"

"Kari?" Damon shrugged as he looked into the fridge for the milk. "Yeah, I think so. She was smiling and looked happy the entire night, that's for sure."

"That's good. What about Sharon? Was she able to go?"

"Yup, she went with Vin."

"That's good she went. I was hoping she had settled in by now and given herself a chance to have some fun. Your mom seems to think she stays in too much for someone so young. Did she have a good time?"

Damon smiled, recalling their dance at the beginning of the night. "Yeah, I'm sure she did."

"Good. Why didn't you ask her again? I thought you liked her."

Damon almost spit out the milk he was drinking. "What!? Who said that?"

Mr. Cardinet allowed a small smile to form on his face, which he hid behind the newspaper. "That's what your mother told me."

"I didn't ask her because Vin already had."

"Would you have asked if he hadn't?"

"I don't know. Maybe?" he answered, trying his best to calm down and get rid of the blush he knew was on his face.

"So you do like her." He allowed the newspaper to drop a little bit so he could look at his eldest child.

"I did not say that."

This time, Mr. Cardinet allowed a small chuckle to escape, causing Damon to blush even harder. "Well, if you think she's worth it, go after her. She seems to be a nice girl, not like what's her name, the girl you went with last night."

"Her name's Kari," Damon frowned a little. "What do you have against her?"

"Nothing," he answered. "She just seems, oh I don't know, a little cold at times. I know you two have grown up and known each other for years and years now, but she's not quite the same, smiling girl I remember from when her family first moved here. These days, she seems ambitious, but not in the best way, if you can understand what I mean. Sharon on the other hand, she seems to be a genuinely nice girl. At least, she has been every time she's come over to babysit Caleb and Ros."

"Huh." Damon took this bit of information and left it at that.

"Well," Mr. Cardinet began as he folded up his newspaper and set it aside. "I'm off to the office again."

"But it's Sunday!"

"I need to take care of some things when there's peace and quiet there. Don't worry. It'll only take a couple of hours. I'll be home long before dinner."

"All right. I'll tell the others when they come down."

"Oh, they're all already out at the park. You do know it's close to noon now, right?"

The blush was back on Damon's face. "I guess I

slept in a bit longer than usual this morning."

"Just don't make it a habit," his father replied, patting his son on the back. "See you in a few hours. Stay out of trouble."

"Yes, Dad," Damon replied as Mr. Cardinet walked out towards the front door.

As soon as the door shut behind him, Damon sighed and lowered his head a little to rub the back of his neck. 'How'd mom know? Even I'm not completely sure how I feel about Sharon. She's a nice girl, yeah, and we get along great. We can definitely talk about anything and do our fair share of teasing and making fun of each other. But was it just me last night or not when it felt like the two of us had been in our own little world when we were dancing together last night? There's no denying the fact that I really enjoyed having her close enough to actually hold her in my arms a couple times. And it just goes to show that whatever physical chemistry between us earlier in the year when we just touched is really there because that electricity was still there last night.'

He sighed again. 'But she went to the dance with Vin. For all I know, he likes her and she feels absolutely nothing for me and likes Vin instead. If only I knew what she was thinking!'

Damon shook his head as if to remove any doubts in his mind. 'No use wondering, D. We'll just see what happens. If we're meant to be together, then it'll happen. If not…'

15

Two weeks later…

"Hello?" Damon called as he swung open the front door to his home. No answer came to him as he shrugged off his backpack in the living room. "Mom? Caleb? Ros?" He walked into the kitchen to check the message board.

It looks like you beat us home. I took Caleb and Ros to the park down the street for a little bit. We'll be back before dark. –Sharon

'Huh, I guess mom isn't done running her errands yet,' he thought as he turned to walk back out the front door.

Regardless of the work out he had gotten in practice that afternoon, Damon found himself ignoring his car in the driveway and jogging down the block towards the park. Despite his best efforts to prevent it, a small smile formed on his face at the thought of seeing Sharon again, and he found himself moving faster towards the park. The smile grew into a broad grin though when he came to the field and found that a mini-football game had sprung up involving his siblings, a few other kids from the local elementary school, and even Sharon while a few of the neighborhood parents watched from the sidelines. Damon himself hung back a moment to watch as the kids ran around, squealing in delight as they ran around with a soft football, more playing keep away from one of the neighbor's dogs who was having a blast running around than really playing football, everyone having fun nonetheless.

He watched as Sharon caught the ball after it had been thrown to her by one of Caleb's classmates. She jogged a few paces forward before allowing herself to be "tackled" by a couple of the kids and the dog. Laughing, she let Ros "steal" the football from her and run towards one end of the field with the prized football clutched tight in her arms. With the attention off of her for the moment, Sharon was able to pick herself up off the ground, gather her hair back into a messy ponytail, and jog slowly back to the action, never once taking her eyes off the kids. She cheered along with everyone else when Ros, by far one of the younger kids playing on the field that day, scored a touchdown and jumped up and down in victory. "Great job, Ros!" she yelled out before another play began.

The smile on Damon's face was a genuine one and after watching a few minutes, felt the urge to join in on the fun himself. He watched as the football sailed in the air a moment and ran forward to catch it.

"Damon!" more than half the kids there cried out when they finally noticed that he was there too. Immediately, they went to tackle the new "big kid" and were successful in bringing the guy down, much to the delight of everyone playing. Still, he managed to keep the ball away from the kids. "Sharon! Here!"

The shock Sharon had gotten from seeing Damon appear almost magically from nowhere dissolved into laughter at the sight of Damon being lost under a pile of kids. His calling her name though, shook her out of her laughter and she easily caught the ball and began running around the field, doing her best to stay just out of reach of the kids who followed her. The dog, however, was not to be outrun and it was its turn to tackle Sharon and bring her to the ground this time. The ball came to Caleb's hands now and he quickly passed it on to one of his friends, who ended up making the last touchdown of the game. With cheers all around, parents slowly gathered up their kids and everyone started making their way home as the sun dipped lower to the horizon and the street lights slowly began to turn on.

Caleb and Ros were still full of energy as they made their way back to the Cardinet household. Caleb was relaying play by play the entire game to Damon while Ros twirled a stick she had found along the way. Only Sharon remained on the quiet side, enjoying the walk as she convinced her heart to slow down, both from the running around and at having Damon so close.

Once inside, Damon sent the two upstairs to wash up before turning back to Sharon. "You're a little quiet, Sharon. You okay?" Damon asked.

She smiled. "I'm fine. Just a little tired I guess from the running. I'm just not used to it anymore," she shrugged.

"Growing up does that sometimes," he smiled back. "Anyway, would you like something to drink before you head home?"

"That's okay," she replied, shaking her head. "I'll just get my stuff together and head on home now that you're here to watch over them. Thanks anyway though, Damon," she added as she went to go pick up her backpack off the living room floor.

"Wait! Do you have to go now?"

"Well, no, I don't technically have to go now, I guess, if you can't take care of your brother and sister on your own…" her eyes twinkled with laughter.

"Haha, very funny!" he retorted, but laughed anyway. "But hang on. I want to make sure I give you something before you leave though." He turned to get his own backpack and, after reaching in, he pulled out an envelope.

"What's this?" she asked, taking the package he was offering to her.

"Those are your homecoming pictures with Vin. He was going to give you your share in the morning but then we remembered that you were babysitting over here this afternoon so he just gave your share to me to give to you. He thought you'd want it."

She smiled as she opened the packet and saw the pictures inside. "Thanks, Damon. That was nice of you to do that."

"Oh! And here," he said, remembering that he had something else to give to her. He reached again into his backpack and pulled out a similar looking envelope. "Here are the group pictures that we got. I didn't have a chance to cut them up and give them out right after school today because of practice, but since you're here now, I may as well give you your share."

"Thank you," she replied, smiling as she looked down at this set of pictures. "Now I can show this to my parents and they can finally put faces to the names I keep giving them." Something though, caught her eye. "Oh no! Riley has his eyes closed in this one!"

Damon started laughing. "Yeah, I noticed that too, but all I can say is I'm glad it's him and not me this time. Somehow, one of us always manages to have our eyes closed in these pictures."

She smiled. "It's still a really good picture though, especially considering how you and the guys cleaned up so well for a dance."

"Look who's talking! You do realize you've just been playing in a field with a bunch of kids and a dog and that you're not exactly the definition of clean right now, right?"

"All the more reason for me to get home and get cleaned up," she laughed. "And besides, now that you're here now, I can go home a little earlier than expected and help out with dinner."

"What about getting paid? Mom should be back soon. I'd give you the money but–"

"Oh, don't worry about it Damon," she brushed it off. "Next time," she smiled and turned toward the door. "Thanks again for the pictures, Damon. I'll see you in school tomorrow."

Once again, she turned towards the door, and this time, Damon couldn't come up with another reason quickly enough to delay her any longer as she yelled out her good-byes to Caleb and Rosaline. With a quick smile and wave, she was out the door and moving towards her car. Damon waved back when she pulled out and headed on home, the smile on his face not fading one bit as he watched her pull away.

16

When Damon finally closed the door a few minutes later, he turned around to find both Caleb and Ros smiling at him from the stairs. "What?"

Caleb only kept smiling before turning to go back upstairs to his room. Ros on the other hand…

"Damon and Sharon, sitting in a tree, K-I-S-S-" she began singing with a goofy grin on her face.

Damon unsuccessfully fought to keep the blush from coming, but come it did, and he found himself running up the stairs to catch his little sister, who ran squealing from him to her room. "Come on, Ros! You know you don't get away from teasing me without getting tickled," he playfully threatened. She only laughed back when he managed to catch her and begin torturing her with tickling. "Mercy?" he asked.

"Never!" she screamed as she tried her best to wriggle out of his grasp.

"Then I'm not going to stop tickling you," he warned.

"Yes, you will."

"Oh really? And what makes you think I'm going to stop tickling you?"

From downstairs, they heard their father call. "Damon?"

Immediately, Damon raised an eyebrow down at his little sister. "Cheater," he smiled.

Ros only stuck out her tongue at him and the two of them left her room to go downstairs.

"Hey, dad! You're home a little earlier than usual."

"Don't get used to it. Unfortunately, until this deal is done, I'm not going to be able to come home before dark too often. Where's Caleb?"

"In his room."

"And Mom?"

"She's still out running errands," Ros supplied.

"Oh. Sharon's gone already?"

"Yup. She only left a few minutes ago."

"Did Mom leave money for her then?"

"Nope."

"You didn't let her leave her without getting paid, did you?" he asked Damon, frowning a little.

"She insisted. When I got home earlier than expected, she really wanted to surprise her own parents by coming home early to help them with dinner and said she can wait until whenever you want to have her over again."

A thoughtful look came across Mr. Cardinet's face as he decided to let the subject drop for the moment. As he turned to go into the kitchen to see what he could start making for dinner, he noticed something though... "Damon, you're looking a little red. Did you have a rough work-out today?"

Immediately, Damon felt his face flush again as he mumbled, "No, not any more than usual..."

Ros burst out laughing and found herself unable to say anything, much to Damon's relief. Caleb, however, chose that moment to stick his head out of his bedroom and call out, "Hi, Dad! Damon's blushing because he likes Sharon and we caught him with a stupid smile on his face after Sharon left."

Damon turned his head to glare at his brother, but Caleb paid him no mind and laughed before ducking back into his room.

"Well, I don't see anything to be embarrassed about. I thought everyone knew that already," Mr. Cardinet stated matter-of-factly, mostly succeeding in hiding his own grin.

"Dad!" Damon exclaimed. "You're not helping things here!"

His father lifted his hands in apology. "Sorry, sorry," he said as he backed his way into the kitchen. "I'll try not to overstep my boundaries next time or suggest you take her out to the movies or get ice-cream at Marty's or something."

"Dad!" This time, Mr. Cardinet just laughed as he retreated into the kitchen to begin preparing dinner. Giggling next to him made Damon turn to Ros next. "And what are you still laughing at?"

"You," she grinned before she skipped her way down the stairs to join her father in the kitchen.

Sighing, Damon made his way up the stairs and into the shower to finally clean off all the dirt and sweat he'd been caked in since practice earlier that afternoon. In the privacy of his room, he was able to forget the teasing from his family, the long day at school and at practice, the amount of homework he had looming in front of him after dinner, the remaining college applications he had left to finish and send out… He pushed all of that out of his mind for the time being to focus on the girl who had caught his eye after their first run-in together.

There was no denying it. The more and more he saw Sharon and spent time with her, the more he wanted to know about her, the more he looked forward to the next time he'd see her, be it at lunch or in class or at home when she was over to babysit Caleb or Ros... It was scaring him that he was starting to look forward more to those few instances than to other things that had meant so much to him in the past.

Damon was falling for Sharon and he didn't know what to do about it.

Sharon was unlike any other girl he'd dated. Most girls in the past had been content with the occasional dinner or movie out, the occasional trips to the park or to the city. Then there were the girls like Kari who considered him to be just a prize, a cute boy to tote around and make her look good. Hers was the kind Damon just didn't understand – didn't they have a bigger ambition than that? Truth be told, he'd only asked Kari to homecoming because he'd waited too long to ask Sharon, and all the other girls he would have asked had made plans already. He knew that Kari had turned down everyone else, risking the lateness in plans in hopes of Damon asking her, and she was rewarded for her patience, a virtue she normally lacked.

Damon sighed. Kari was nowhere near what he wanted in a girl and secretly agreed with his father's disapproval of 'that' kind of girl. He was just more tolerant than his father with those types of things because there just wasn't anything he could do about it. Still, he did find it interesting that his father hadn't been too fond of any of his female friends, save Ana and now Sharon.

Ana he understood. She and Damon had practically grown up together just down the street from each other, and they'd always been naturally close. They were always honest with each other, and were always willing to help each other out in their times of need. She'd been there to help him cope years ago when his favorite grandmother had died and he couldn't talk to anyone else about it. He was there for her when her first boyfriend left her heartbroken.

Damon knew people were surprised that the two of them hadn't ended up together. After all, they knew each other's faults and compensated with their strengths. Hopes and fears were not a secret between the two, and they often pushed each other to reach their dreams, helping each other achieve the most out of what life had given them. This, he knew, was important for his father. The fact that Ana had aspirations and the motivation to become a doctor after college was important. Kari... just didn't have it all together yet.

He knew he was blessed to have such a good, true friend as Ana, but he also knew that he was genuinely happy for the relationship she shared with Riley. Those two reminded him a lot of her parents and even his own to a certain extent. They just worked well together.

And Damon knew that that was what he wanted in the end. He wasn't going to settle for anything else otherwise – it just wouldn't be worth it.

He wasn't certain if Sharon would be the one for him yet, but he was certain that she was the best girl out there for him at the moment because frankly, no one else at the school met his standards. The fact that his family had taken such an immediate liking to her was also a big deal to Damon, especially when considering the fact that they usually remained more on the reserved side whenever he brought company home (except for his mother, who was just a naturally an open, accepting, and outgoing person), and it never occurred to him as anything strange until he thought about how differently they treated Sharon. With her, they were definitely more open – Ros had dropped the shy act as soon as Sharon had been there with the band-aid incident a couple of months ago. Caleb had taken longer to warm up to Sharon being even shyer than Ros, but in the end, he had also opened up to her in his own way. Now, his two siblings were always looking forward to when Sharon would come over to babysit – they'd never responded as well or as quickly to any other sitter in the past outside of family.

And if that was a miracle, it was even more so with Damon's dad regularly asking about Sharon now. He may not be home consistently due to his work, but he still managed to stay on top of things that involved his family. That meant also knowing his children's business. Damon considered himself lucky that he had an open, honest relationship with his dad, who always shared his views on one person or another when he was alone with his son, and rarely ever warmed up to any of his friends except those closest to Damon.

'Like father, like son,' Damon mused. While both

men were well-liked among their respective peers, they were also mindful of the company they found themselves with. They knew better than to talk too candidly with the likes of Kari, but also knew to treasure the lasting relationships, like the one Mr. Cardinet had with his wife and the friendships Damon shared with Ana and Riley and a few others.

And for some reason, Damon had instinctively trusted Sharon and placed her in that exclusive group. Again, that was a feat in its own right. It normally took Damon a long time to establish friendships, not necessarily because he didn't trust people, but more because he wanted to have his trust earned, and that took time.

Sharon was different, and he knew it the moment she stepped into the high school. When he had first noticed her hesitating just inside the main doors and orienting herself to her surroundings, he had also noticed a kind of strength to her, almost like she'd been through it all and had lived to tell her tale. Whatever that history was, and he admitted to himself that he didn't know much about that part of her yet, it had done nothing to take away from how he felt about her. This was a woman with a story, and he'd been drawn to her from the start.

Damon sighed as he got ready to go back downstairs for dinner. Admitting to himself that he liked Sharon had been difficult to swallow… Ana had actually been the one to finally get him to admit it out loud weeks ago, and this was another secret they shared. Still, if Sharon was as special as he thought her to be and suspected her to be, he didn't want to ruin whatever friendship they had by doing anything stupid.

"*Damon,*" Ana had told him when she'd confronted him about his feelings for Sharon. "*Nothing's wrong with asking a girl out to get to know her.*"

"*I know,*" he had replied. "*But I don't want to rush things. She just moved here and is still settling in.*"

"*That's such a bad excuse, even for you.*"

One thing about being so close, they knew all the buttons to push to get each other aggravated. That was one such moment and he'd scowled at Ana for being right.

"*Just ask her out, Damon. If you don't, someone else will, and trust me, it won't take long. I've seen how some of the guys look at her like fresh meat. Just because she hangs out with us doesn't give her complete immunity to other guys who want to try their luck.*"

A week later, Vin asked Sharon to go with him to homecoming and Ana had given Damon a knowing look. He hadn't needed her to say out loud that she'd already "told him so."

"As if things weren't hard enough as it already is," he muttered to himself as he made his way downstairs. "Still, we'll see how things turn out in the end. Things may change for the better yet."

An image of a dragon crossed his mind and he smiled. Those magical creatures that he had dreamt of as a child represented strength and power, both of which he knew he had and suspected would help him get what he wanted. He just needed the right situation…

17

"You lied to me!"

Those were the first words she heard after Sharon had said hello into the phone later that night. "Kelly! What are you talking about now?"

"The picture! What else would I be talking about?"

"But I just sent that scan five minutes ago!"

"And I just happened to be online when you did that. Sharon, what's holding you back? He's gorgeous!"

"Vin?"

"Damon! Although true, Vin's not at all bad on the eyes, but Damon's hot!"

Sharon burst out laughing at Kelly's bluntness and couldn't stop for the next couple of minutes. It was bad enough that Kelly couldn't even get a word in. Eventually though, she was able to calm down enough to catch her breath. "I'm sorry. I didn't mean to go off like that. Still, I'm confused. What did I lie to you about?"

"Okay, maybe you didn't lie to me," she conceded. "But you deliberately did not tell me how cute Damon really is!" Kelly replied with a soft 'hmph!' "And I just don't see how this can be so amusing to you because I'm serious, Shar. Why haven't you asked him out yet?"

"Hello? It's not proper for a girl to ask a guy out

for a date," she found herself replying quickly.

"I didn't say date! What's stopped you from asking someone to hang out with you before? You haven't even tried to make any attempt whatsoever. Why not?"

"Because I haven't?"

"I got that, yes, but why not!? Do you really need me to give you my blessing and tell you that it's all right to move on and date a nice, cute, smart guy like Damon?"

"Geez, you don't have to spell it out for me."

"As your best friend, I am entitled to do so whenever you don't listen to me!"

"I'm listening right now!"

"Right… Then hang up on me right now, call Damon, and ask him to go with you to the movies tomorrow night."

"I can't."

"And why not?"

"Because he's having dinner with his family right now," she replied with a quick glance at the clock. "And he has an away game tomorrow night and won't be back in town until late."

"Now you're just making excuses and you know it," Kelly accused.

"But both points are true. Besides, what if he doesn't like me like that?"

Kelly bit back a frustrated scream on her side. "We've been through this time and time again. How will you ever find out if you never even try and ask?" Kelly moaned.

"But I don't want to get hurt again."

"Sharon, not every guy out there is like Patrick,"

she said sternly. She heard Sharon breathe in sharply and sighed. "You know I'm right," she added quieter.

After a pause, Sharon replied, "Yes, I know that."

"Listen, have you at least talked to Ana or someone yet? Maybe she can help you out."

"No, I haven't talked to anyone about that yet. Maybe later," she answered vaguely.

"You know, it's a good thing I'm coming down to visit you in a couple of weeks. I don't know what's happened to you since you left here but you're holding back in a way that's not you. On one hand, you know how to control yourself better since you're able to step back and think about the big picture more. On the other hand, I think that control is making you over-analyze and stop things before they even have a chance to start. We all get hurt, Sharon, and that's a fact of life. It's how we pick ourselves up and move on that's important."

"Gee, thanks for making me sound like a nut case here," Sharon smiled a little.

This time, Kelly didn't bite back her scream. "You haven't listened to a word I just said!"

"On the contrary, I was listening. I just don't want to admit it to myself that you're right and I'm just going crazy over a stupid boy when just a couple of months ago, I'd sworn off guys entirely."

"Hey, one of us has to be going crazy at any given moment. It just happens to be your lucky day today."

"Funny, and I thought I was perfectly sane before I got on the phone with you."

"What can I say? I bring that out in people,"

Kelly laughed.

"And that makes me wonder why guys ever think of dating you."

"Hey!"

"I'm kidding!" Sharon laughed.

"Yeah right! You know, I bet you would just be a lot happier if you even just found out if Damon was seeing someone seriously or not. At least that would be one question out of the way and then you can move on from there."

"Mm, we'll see. How about this though? If nothing changes by the time you get down here, I'll give you free reign, within reason, to try your luck on me."

"Are you serious? You'd give me complete freedom?" she asked, not believing she'd heard right.

Sharon laughed. "It just means I have to do something soon to prevent any embarrassing moments from taking place while you're around."

"Somehow, I have the feeling that will happen regardless of my involvement or not," Kelly teased. "Still, I think you're on. I accept your challenge. Question is, will you honor your part and actually try something before I get there? I don't want to do all of the work here, you know."

"I promise I'll try my best," came the coy response.

Kelly sighed. "Well, I guess I'll have to take it. That's better than nothing."

"Of course. Now, what did you think about the rest of the picture?"

"Other than the fact that Kari ruined it by trying

and failing at pulling off the oh-look-I'm-so-mature, serious pose by not smiling when everyone else was?" she laughed. "I swear, she looked so stiff and pouty... I bet she wanted that homecoming crown for herself to go with that royal, egotistic vibe I was getting off of just looking at her."

Sharon laughed. "You pick that and not Riley's eyes being closed?"

"It gives him character, and at least he's smiling. Kari just looks fake."

"Well, I'll be honest and say that her name was on the ballot for homecoming queen now that you mention it, but Ana won by a landslide. She's just that popular and nice to boot."

"Then you should talk to Ana! If she's even half as nice as you make her sound and as close to Damon as I think you're hinting at, I bet she'd be more than willing to at least talk to you about him, at least give a little bit of his background on the guy. Besides, I have a feeling I'm going to need back up when I'm down there."

"Uh oh... Back up for what?"

"Nothing to worry your pretty little mind over."

"And that doesn't help me one bit, knowing you're already scheming things in your mind."

"You did give me free reign," she reminded Sharon.

"Yes, and don't make me take it back. I did say within reason."

"And would I do anything to embarrass you?" Kelly asked innocently.

"Do you really need me to answer that one?" Sharon laughed back. "Let's see, there was the time when you pasted pictures of certain male pop stars all over my yearbook last year and I had to explain to the teachers what those were about when they gave me strange looks before signing it."

Kelly laughed. "Oh, but that was so much fun! I think that's one of my best works of art, to be honest."

"Oh really? I'm sure you think that way, but I'm telling you that I don't think Mr. Wilder or any of the others will ever think of me quite the same."

"That was partially the idea."

"Remind me later that I have to repay you in kind someday."

"Good luck trying," came the reply, sending both girls laughing.

18

'I knew I shouldn't have had that mocha before school!' Sharon thought to herself after her first morning class the next day. She had left the classroom for the bathroom as soon as the bell had rung. 'I could barely sit still during that test!'

As she bent forward at the sink to finish washing her hands, she found herself catching a conversation in the background…

"I mean, come on!" She recognized the voice as Kari's. "You think Damon and I would make a good-looking couple, don't you? Just look at the pictures!"

"I saw the pictures and I agree. What guy wouldn't want to go out with you?" Sharon heard in the undertone, however, the girl's exasperation and sarcasm, as if they'd had this conversation too many times for the other girl's taste.

"Exactly!" Kari replied, apparently not hearing the same tones Sharon had. "I mean, what can any other girl give him that I don't have? Especially that new girl, what's her name."

"Oh, I don't know… Sharon seems nice. A little quiet maybe, but that's certainly nothing to go crazy about. Besides, maybe Damon's just not interested in you."

"What? You did not just say that! The next thing I know, you'll say he probably likes her over me.

Yeah right!" Kari was laughing, not taking the other female seriously.

Sharon smiled as she left the bathroom.

"You're in a good mood."

She turned her head to the left and noticed Vin walking next to her. "Yeah, I am. I think I did pretty well on my first government test, and I just heard something highly amusing."

"What was that?"

"I can't say. Have you seen Ana around?"

"Oh I see how it is. This is one of your girl things," he rolled his eyes and laughed.

"You're quick to assume," she pointed out, smiling.

"Am I wrong?"

"No, you're not," she conceded.

Again, Vin laughed. "Anyway, to answer your question, no, I haven't seen Ana, at least not since before school. She's in my next class though. Do you want me to pass along the message that you're looking for her?"

"No, don't worry about it. It's not important. I'll just ask her later."

"All right. Anyway, I want to ask you something."

"Sure. What's up, Vin?"

"Well, I was just wondering if you were free tonight."

"What's going on?"

"I just thought it might be nice for you to come along and cheer for us at our game tonight."

Sharon smiled. "I'll keep it in mind and ask my parents if I can go. Same time as always?"

"Yup, and we're playing against a team in the next town, so it's not far away at all."

"Got it. I'll let you know." Sharon waved bye to Vin as she ducked into her next class and he made his way further down the hall. She moved easily to her seat towards the back of her calculus class and pointedly didn't look up when Kari entered just a few moments later. Sharon was still smiling, and she didn't want Kari's scowling face ruining her morning.

Halfway through class, she was still in good spirits. She could care less that she could sense Kari often glancing her way to glare at her when their teacher wasn't looking, but she was starting to find it a little distracting and more than a little annoying, and so she resolved herself to do something about it after class.

As soon as the bell rang, Sharon quickly gathered her things and rushed to catch the girl. Within a few strides, she had easily caught up with the blonde. "Hey, Kari."

Kari turned to her, surprised. "You're talking to me?" The look on her face was one of disbelief.

"Yeah. Listen, I was just wondering, have I done something wrong against you?"

Kari looked at her as if she were the idiot. "Are you that stupid?" she laughed.

Sharon fought the urge to roll her eyes. "Humor me."

"No. If you haven't figured it out, you're just hopeless, princess. Now listen, I don't ever want to talk to you again. I don't like you."

And with that, Kari stalked off, eager to

dissociate herself from Sharon as quickly as possible. 'So much for making things better. Oh well. At least I tried.' Sharon shrugged it off and turned back the way she had come to get her lunch from her locker.

- - -

Damon cocked his head a little at the sight in front of him down the hall. He just couldn't believe that Sharon and Kari were talking. Riley couldn't believe it either. "What do you suppose that's about, Damon?"

"I have no idea." The memory of Kari snubbing Sharon during homecoming came to mind, and he couldn't understand why Sharon had bothered to initiate a talk with the other girl.

"Maybe they have a project together?"

"In calculus? I doubt it."

"How'd you know they were in math?" Riley turned to his friend.

"They walked out of Ms. Davison's class," he returned easily, ignoring the fact that he also knew Sharon's schedule by heart. "Anyway, come on." He and Riley ducked out of the main doors to go claim their table for lunch just as Sharon was turning their way.

"Well, whatever that was about, Kari sure didn't look too happy about it. Did you see how she stomped off like that?"

Damon indicated that he had seen and turned to head to the lunch line after dropping off his backpack at their table. 'Well, you did say she had her secrets, D,' he thought. 'We'll just wait and see what that was all about later, I guess.'

- - -

Out of the corner of her eye, she noticed Ana making her way down the hall and out to lunch. Sharon quickly finished at her locker and slammed it shut before racing over. "Hey, Ana. I have a question for you."

Ana looked over to Sharon and smiled. "Oh hey, Sharon. Vin mentioned that you wanted to talk to me. What's up?"

"It's just that, well, what's the deal with Kari?"

Ana looked over at Sharon out of the corner of her eye. "Deal?"

She shrugged. "She doesn't like me, even though I don't think I've given her any reason to think or act like that. I actually just tried asking her about it during break, but she just brushed me away. I'm just wondering if I did something wrong."

Ana smiled. "You're a lot more patient and nice than I thought. Honestly, I'm very surprised you even gave her the time of day. Kari…" She paused for a moment, trying to figure out the best way to put this. "I'll give you the condensed version. She's the center of her universe. Her parents spoiled her like crazy since she's an only child and they still do, so she has this strange notion of living in a perfect world where the only opinion that matters is her own and her needs are more important than anyone else's. That being said, she only wants the best for herself, and that includes getting Damon to call her boyfriend. Thankfully, he's not interested in her and has the brains to realize why she's not his type. Kari, however, just doesn't get it.

"As for where you come in, I'm assuming that because she's been seeing you guys talking more with each other than she does with him, she thinks you're probably after him too, and that makes you a threat." Was it her imagination or did Sharon blush slightly just then? Ana kept that observation to herself as she continued.

"Don't worry about her. She's really harmless. She just gets insanely jealous when she doesn't get what she wants. That's why she won't speak with me either. A, I'm too close to Damon for her comfort, and B, I'm head cheerleader and she isn't," she smiled.

Sharon just shook her head. "That's so stupid though. Who'd want to hang on to all that drama?"

"What can I say? As much as I hate stereotypes, I honestly believe she's just blonde through and through, and definitely no one to lose sleep over."

"I guess…"

"Anyway, are you going to the game tonight?" Ana asked, changing the subject.

"I don't know. Maybe. Vin reminded me that it's an away game today."

"You should go! It'll be fun. Hey, I can even drive you if you want."

"Really? But I thought you had to ride in with the guys."

"Sometimes we do, but usually not. It's not pleasant riding with a bus full of guys, especially after a game when they're all hot and smelly," she laughed.

Sharon had to agree, the thought of it was definitely not a good one. "Well then, if my parents agree and you really don't mind driving, I don't see why not. I'll talk to my parents after school and give you a call later today."

"Okay, that's fine by me," she answered as the two sat down at the table the guys had found and saved this time.

"Ladies," Riley acknowledged them as they sat down. "How are you doing this fine, Friday morning?"

"Just fine," Ana answered for the both of them, before leaning in to give Riley a quick kiss. "Your morning going okay so far?"

"But of course," he smiled, wrapping an arm comfortably around Ana's shoulders.

Sharon smiled a little at the sight the two made. Ever since homecoming night, it'd become more and more clear that Ana was dating Riley and not Damon. Ana and Damon definitely acted more like siblings – close, but not in love with each other romantically. With Riley, Ana was definitely more affectionate, and Sharon found it absolutely adorable how those two kept on surprising each other with the littlest things. Today, he'd found a purple flower of some kind and Ana was now wearing it, tucked behind one ear.

She looked up and found Damon walking in their direction with a tray of food in hand. She grinned at him, but inwardly, she sighed a little. 'Ana and Riley look so happy together. Will I be able to share that happiness someday with Damon? We'll see…' she thought as Damon walked closer.

– – –

Damon caught Sharon's smile and instantly grinned back. He set his tray down and took the empty seat next to Sharon as she turned to answer a question one of their other friends had just asked. He ignored his food for a moment to reach into his backpack. Without pulling it out, he fingered the object he sought and debated whether or not to give it to Sharon then and there. Taking a quick look around the table though, he decided that this wasn't the right time. 'Next period, in art,' he thought to himself, knowing much less fuss and attention would be given then.

19

"Hey Kelly," Sharon answered quickly as she hopped around her room trying to find the matching sneaker to the one she was wearing now. "I can't talk. I'm heading out."

"You had the guts to talk to Damon?"

"Not yet. I'm just going to their game tonight and show my support, but I can't find my shoe and Ana's coming any second now to pick me up."

"Look at you, showing your school spirit," Kelly laughed. "Or is it that your ultimate goal is to check Damon out behind his back?"

"You are impossible," Sharon stated matter-of-factly.

"Well, have you gotten anywhere?"

"I found out that he doesn't find Kari to be his type of girl."

"Ooh, that's a step in the right direction. How'd you find that out?"

"Ana and I had a little talk after I'd tried to make nice with Kari, or at least get her to tell me what she had against me."

Kelly laughed. "Only you would do something like that. Was I right in saying she thought you were competition?"

"Not surprisingly, yes, you were. I just wanted to give her the benefit of the doubt, you know?"

"Still, at least you know that now. How are

things on the Damon front directly?"

"Nothing's changed. Must you ask this every night?"

"Every night you don't do anything is another night closer to when I get down there and get the chance to stir things up."

"Well don't get your hopes set too high just yet. You have a couple of weeks left until Thanksgiving break and things can happen in the meantime."

"We'll see about that."

A knock at the front door signaled Ana's arrival. "Okay, I gotta go. Ana's here."

"All right. I'll talk to you tomorrow."

"Bye." Sharon hung up the phone and quickly grabbed a purse and heading out. "Good night!" she called out to her parents before exiting her home. "Hey Ana!"

"Ready to go?" her friend smiled.

"Yup," she answered as she locked the front door behind her.

"Then let's go!" The two got into Ana's car and were soon on their way out of the neighborhood and into the main streets that would take them over to the highway.

A few minutes into the ride, Sharon asked, "Who's this on the radio right now?" Ana told her and Sharon nodded to herself. "Good beat."

Ana smiled. "It's a great way to get the blood pumping pre-game."

Sharon couldn't help but agree as she and Ana both found themselves singing along with the chorus.

Soon, another song came on, only this time

slower and quieter, giving Ana the chance to glance over at Sharon a moment before returning her eyes to the road. "So, Sharon, I'm curious… Are you single?"

"Where'd that come from?" she asked, smiling as she turned to look at Ana.

"Curious minds want to know."

"Minds?" Ana just smiled and waited for Sharon to answer. "Fine. Yes, I'm not seeing anyone right now." Ana's smile grew wider. "I broke up with my last boyfriend just before I moved down here."

"He couldn't handle the long distance?"

"You could say that," she replied vaguely. "He couldn't handle separation in general," she added before stopping, uncomfortable about sharing anymore for the moment.

Ana wasn't insensitive to her feelings and dropped that part of the topic for now. "Well, at least you're single. Has anyone caught your eye?"

Sharon was glad that they were in the dark and she could hide the slight coloring in her cheeks. "Oh, I don't know…"

"Come on, I won't tell a soul, I promise."

Sharon laughed. "You sound just like my best friend back home. I think you guys would totally get along with each other and end up ganging up on me or something." In the back of her mind, she remembered Kelly's threat to join forces with Ana should things not progress for Sharon.

Ana smiled. "I bet she knows who you like."

"Of course," she answered before realizing what she'd confessed to.

"A-ha! You do like someone! Tell me! Maybe I

can help out!"

"Uh uh," Sharon laughed. "I don't think I'm quite ready for the dating world yet."

"You may not be, but I know guys who are dying to go out with you."

"Guys?" she emphasized the plural, disbelieving.

"Don't tell me you haven't noticed all the attention you've gotten since you've been here."

"No, I haven't noticed, mostly because I've been trying not to. It's just because I'm the new girl, huh?"

Ana nodded. "Most of them are good guys though, so no worries there. And you can trust me on that, seeing how I've grown up with most of these people over the years."

Sharon let this info sink in before turning her head to look out the window. "Well, I'll be honest about one thing. If ever I do go back into the dating world, I hope it's with one of the good guys."

Ana looked over at Sharon with a curious look on her face, but Sharon wasn't going to give any more details that night. With a slight shrug, Ana let the subject drop completely and focused on the road ahead of her.

- - -

With a quick wave, Ana left Sharon at the guest stands to join her fellow cheerleaders on the field. Sharon turned around and looked for a place to sit. She found an open area towards one side of the bleachers and was about to head over there when she heard voices calling her name. "Sharon!! Sharon, over here!"

Puzzled, she turned in the direction that the voices were coming from. 'Maybe they mean someone else?' she thought at first when she couldn't find the source, but no, it happened to be Damon's mom and Ros calling over to her. She smiled and waved and then watched as Ros started moving towards her. "Hey, princess. How are you?" she asked as soon as she got closer to her.

"Good," she said, grabbing onto her hand and then dragging her over to where her mother sat in the stands.

"Hi, Mrs. Cardinet. How are you?"

"Very well, dear. And how are you?" Mrs. Cardinet patted the space next to her, inviting her to join them.

"I'm doing all right. Where's Caleb?" she questioned.

"He's with his father at the stand getting us some food. They should be back shortly."

"That's good that Mr. Cardinet was able to make it."

"Indeed, it has been good having him home more often."

Sharon turned her head then to look back at Ros and noticed she was looking at her hands intently, but not wanting to draw attention to herself. Sharon smiled and pulled up the left sleeve of her sweater slightly to show the friendship bracelet Ros had made, thinking also of how Damon had approached her with it.

They were in art class again, working together on

their latest project. "Remember class, I want to see what is important to you in this world, see what the world is like for you, through your eyes. Incorporate the things that are important to you in your models," Mr. Flynn was reminding them all as he walked around the room to view the progress.

Sharon was working on creating another clay, spiral ribbon to attach to the base that Damon was working on. "You know, the sketch we made looks so much simpler than it really is to make."

"No kidding. Next time, we'll leave out your details and additions and stick with my simple stick figures. I still think a bunch of circles would have been fine, but no, you want to go all out for this project," he teased.

"Oh please, like we as teens are really constrained to just circles when we're really trying to push our boundaries."

"Ahh, boundaries," he smiled as he continued working on shaping the human head in front of him. "It's you and Ana who think that we should make something of ourselves during our senior year."

"As if you're not doing the very same thing yourself," she retorted, but smiled anyway. "So what'd you bring for your contribution to the project?"

He paused from his sculpting to grab his backpack. "Here," he said, taking out small models of a graduation cap and diploma, a stethoscope, and a football. He laid those on the table, and she nodded her head, taking her own backpack and pulling out a pencil, a small pillow with a message sewn onto it, a blank CD, and a small piece of chain link. He questioned her with a look.

"The pencil is for my drawings, the CD is for music," she explained. "The pillow is something my friends gave *me before I left, and the chain…" He noticed a tightness to her features that he'd never seen before as she struggled to find a way to explain it… But she couldn't. She shook her head. "It's a broken chain," she said flatly, ignoring his eyes.*

Without recognizing what he was doing, Damon lifted a hand to rest over one of hers in comfort and gave it a little squeeze. She smiled a little at the gesture before drawing her hand away. Unhappy with the sudden loss of contact, he reached back down into his backpack and finally drew out the bracelet Ros had made for her. "Here," he said, handing her the bracelet.

The tightness left Sharon's face, and she looked at the bracelet in question. "What's this?"

"Ros made it and wanted you to have it. She's getting to like you a lot, you know."

Immediately, Sharon smiled, and any last trace of uneasiness left her. "How sweet!" she said, putting it on immediately.

"Sharon, Damon," Mr. Flynn's voice addressed the two, interrupting their talk. "Interesting work. Keep at it," he said before moving on.

"Tell her thank you for me," she said lowly as they resumed their work.

"Of course I will. I'm glad you like it."

"You're wearing it!" Ros exclaimed happily.

"Of course I am," she smiled widely. "And I want to thank you personally for making me such a beautiful bracelet. It was very thoughtful of you," she finished, bending down and giving the younger girl a hug.

Sharon watched as Ros blushed a deep, red color.

'So like her brother,' she smiled inwardly.

"Sharon!" she turned to watch as a few of her friends walked over and settled down in the row in front of them. "Hey, Mrs. Cardinet!" they greeted Damon's mom. "Hey Ros!" The little girl smiled shyly at the others and wrapped her arms tightly around her mother's. "Hello everyone. How are your parents?" Mrs. Cardinet asked each one as they all settled in.

A few moments later, Caleb and Mr. Cardinet joined them in the bleachers, arms loaded with popcorn, soda, hot dogs, candy... "Sharon!" Caleb beamed and Sharon said her hello to him as she stood to help the boys out with the food.

"A little hungry?" she teased Caleb.

"It's tradition," he answered back as he sat down. "Here," he said, offering her some candy. He tossed a bag of gummi bears to his sister and sat down to watch as the teams started assembling out onto the field.

"Perfect timing," Mrs. Cardinet was saying.

"Every time," her husband replied back. "It's nice to see you again, Sharon. How are you today?"

"I'm fine." Before she could say anymore however, the announcer chose that moment to begin introducing the teams, and Sharon felt herself sit back to watch the game with the rest of the crowd.

20

"Well good morning, sweetie!"

"Good morning," Sharon replied, greeting her mother with a kiss on the cheek. "Where's dad?" she asked as she got out some cereal and poured herself a bowl.

"Oh, he was on call at the hospital and actually got called in to help out early this morning. I think one of the other nurses called in sick."

"Okay. And are you going in to work at the office also later?"

Her mother smiled. "Nope. I have this weekend off. Do you have any sitting jobs this weekend?"

Sharon frowned briefly as she thought about what she had going on for her this weekend. "No, actually I don't think I have anything planned besides the usual schoolwork."

"Good. How about a girl's day out?"

Sharon smiled. "We haven't done that in ages."

"My thoughts exactly. So what do you say? Are you up to it?"

"Of course! You know you don't have to ask me that one twice," Sharon grinned.

Within an hour, both women were strolling downtown window-shopping. They walked at an easy pace, Sharon's arm linked with her mother's. "How about this store?" Mrs. Werner suggested, pointing to a gift store towards their right.

"Sure. I think I can get some more of my Christmas shopping done while we're here."

"And who else are you shopping for now? I thought you were done."

"Just because I started my shopping early doesn't mean I'm done. I'm just taking full advantage of the fact that Kelly's coming down so I can pack her up with stuff to give to Jan and Ivana for me so I don't have to send those up separately and risk them getting damaged."

"Opportunist."

"I'd like to say practical," Sharon smiled sweetly. They shopped quietly for a while, her mother going over to look at some holiday cards while Sharon browsed the figurine collections. Sharon picked up one figurine of a girl in a graduation gown and ended up putting that down. 'That's not quite the right gift for Jan...' A little further down the shelf though, she saw that same girl dressed in a doctor's coat and pointing to an eye chart; the patient was a stuffed bunny sitting a little lopsided in the patient chair. Sharon smiled. 'Bingo! All right, another part of her gift is done. What about Ivana though...'

"Sharon? What do you think of this?"

She walked over to where her mother was standing a few feet away, took one look at the object in her mother's hand, and started laughing. Just as quickly, she tried to quiet herself down, noticing how a few of the nearby customers had turned in their direction. "Mom, this is perfect for Ivana! Here, she thinks I've gone all country and rural on her, well I'll just give her a taste of it herself."

Her mother smiled. "My thoughts exactly," she

143

said, placing the goofy-looking, stuffed cow in the basket Sharon was holding. "Nice choice for Jan too," she added with a quick glance at the figurine already inside.

"You know us too well," Sharon kidded.

Her mother shrugged. "It's a mother's job to know all… Or at least we pretend to," she replied as she hugged her daughter. "Have you talked to them lately?" she asked as they separated.

"Well, I talked to Kelly last night for a little bit before I left for the game. I spoke with Ivana the other night to catch up too. Jan and I have been doing more of the whole e-mail thing because we can never quite catch each other on the phone, but it sounds like everyone's doing well for the most part. Anyway, did you find any cards?"

"No, not yet. I think I'll wait until it's a little closer to Thanksgiving before I get those."

"It's coming up."

"And I can hold out until then," she smiled. "Have you finished your shopping for Kelly?"

"Some of it, but I don't think I'll find anything else in here for her."

"All right, let's go pay then. Maybe we'll have some better luck at another store."

"What about you? Have you found stuff for your friends back up north?"

"Not really. I haven't had time to really look."

"Mom, what else are we doing today besides shopping?"

"Don't be sarcastic with me, young lady," she laughed. "I'm looking, trust me. I just haven't found anything yet."

"Do you still talk to them?"

"A few of them, yes. Others… Well, you know how it is. Difficult times on top of distance often show you who your true friends are."

Sharon silently agreed as she paid for her friends' gifts.

"So are you going to get anything for your friends here?"

"Probably. At least for Ana-"

"And Damon too, right?" her mother interjected quickly.

Sharon felt some heat come on her face. "I'm thinking about it."

"Now tell me, Sharon," she started as they walked out the door. "What's going on with this Damon boy?"

"What do you mean? Nothing's going on."

"Exactly! At the beginning of the school year, it was all about this new boy. Damon was nice, he was funny, he welcomed you and introduced you to his friends, he got you to go to the welcome dance, etc., etc., etc. You're babysitting his siblings, his family is great, and they seem to really like you. And don't even try to hide and say you're not interested in him anymore because I hear how you talk about him to Kelly."

"Mom!"

"Mother's duty to pry," she smiled.

"You're lucky I love you because otherwise I'd be offended," Sharon laughed. "Really, you sound just like Kelly. Why are you guys so interested in this working out?"

"We just want you to be happy, sweetie. You

know, after Patrick and the issues you had with him, you can only imagine the relief your friends and family have when we hear that you're interested in someone who treats you well."

"Well I certainly appreciate the sentiment, but I'm fine. I like him, I admit that, but I'm still not going to risk my happiness of just settling in and finding people I can hang around with and be happy with because they don't know my drama just to get together with one of those friends."

"Does he like you?"

Sharon laughed. "I am and forever will be oblivious to that unless it's right in my face. You know I'm just hopeless in that regard."

"And I think you're just lying. Surely you have some indication, if not Damon but someone else. What about Vin?"

"Vin's a nice guy, but I'm not interested in him."

"Does he know that? Because he seemed pretty interested in you when he was over the night of your homecoming dance."

"And how could you tell that?"

"Don't tell me you've lost the ability to notice when a guy won't stop staring at you. His eyes were positively glued to you after you walked in the room. You should have seen the look on your father's face."

Sharon laughed again. "Even if that were the case, there's no electricity between us, not like between Damon and I. Vin's just a friend."

"Is Damon single?" her mother asked suddenly.

"Unless he met someone last night after the game or this morning, then yes, he's single."

"So what's holding you back, Sharon?"

"Lack of time due to school and babysitting? Common friends? Settling in?"

"Those are just excuses."

"Well, what about the whole I don't want to get hurt again, or have my friendships ruined, or force my family to move again because of a stupid mistake that I make?"

Her mother was silent for awhile. "Have you told anyone here what happened?"

"No," she replied just as quietly. "The past is history. There's no need to bring it up here."

"Haven't people questioned?"

"People ask, but I don't tell them much. I just say there were circumstances and we ended up relocating here, end of story. They don't need to hear all that past."

Mrs. Werner nodded. "I suppose you're right. What matters is that we're here and happy, right?"

"Right," Sharon agreed, pushing painful memories out of her mind as the two walked on.

21

"SHARON!!"

Sharon stopped her pacing and immediately ran to meet her best friend as she raced from the terminal. A moment later, Kelly and Sharon were laughing as they embraced, ignoring the looks other people were shooting their way.

"You're finally here!!" Sharon exclaimed.

"Yes, I finally am. Oh Sharon, it's so good to see you again. How are things?" she asked, finally breaking away and picking up the backpack she'd dropped just before the hug.

"Things are fine and well. Did you check anything in?"

"Of course! A week's worth of clothes and gifts from Jan and Ivana all don't fit in one backpack."

"Silly me, what was I thinking?"

"Obviously, you weren't," Kelly teased as they walked over to the luggage claim, arms linked together. "So has anything changed?"

Sharon groaned. "No, and yes, it's because I didn't try."

"When do I meet him?" she asked, getting straight to the point.

"Depending on the traffic, either before or after tonight's football game."

"Good. The sooner, the better. That way, I have more time to work my magic."

"You're determined to go through with this, huh?"

"It's one of the reasons why I'm here. Besides, when we look back on this five years from now, I bet you'll be thanking me for this."

"Right, if I haven't died from utter humiliation by the end of the week."

"Car crashes, plane crashes, and a bunch of other things, maybe. But I don't think it's been clinically proven that humiliation can kill a person."

"Fine, then I'll be the first and I can have you to blame."

"Sharon!" Kelly laughed. "Why are you so against this?"

"I am not. I'm just really scared of the ideas you have going on in that head of yours."

"Oh come on. Like I'd really do anything to embarrass you."

The two girls looked at each other for a moment and then burst out laughing.

"Okay, maybe I would," Kelly conceded. "But you know that it's all in fun."

"Oh, I know that. I think the only reason why I put up with it is because it is you and I trust you."

"Well I should hope so considering we've been friends for close to eight years now."

"And there's not a day that goes by that I'm not thankful for having you around."

"Why Sharon, you're getting all sentimental on me," she said with an attempt at a Southern drawl and wave of a hand.

"Well Kelly, you ended up in the hospital because of me," she replied solemnly.

"Stop it right there Sharon. This is the last time we are ever going to talk about this, okay, and I'm only doing this now because we didn't get to see each other face to face to talk about this earlier." She stopped in her tracks and forcibly turned Sharon so they could look each other in the eye. "Everything that happened before you moved here happened for a reason. If anything else, all the craziness that went on with Patrick showed you how people who truly care for you should act and what people who don't value you should not be allowed to do to you, ever. Yes, people were hurt, mostly emotionally, you and I physically, but we've healed or are healing in your case. We all have survived, all of us, including you. If I hadn't been there, you know things could have turned out much different and we wouldn't be here today. Therefore, I refuse to give in to any pity or guilty feelings or whatever. I don't regret anything and neither should you."

Sharon shrugged, breaking eye contact. "Give me five years for that one. It's not every day that we all go through that kind of trauma, you know."

Kelly sighed as she turned back to the luggage carousel. "As true as that is, I hope it doesn't take you five years. As much as you can, try to let this go, okay? We're all rooting for you and we know you've got this," she stated as she pulled her suitcase off the conveyor belt and onto the floor. With a snap, she tugged the handle up and linked her other arm back with Sharon. Silently, Sharon nodded and started directing them out towards the parking garage to get to the car.

- - -

Damon greeted the crowd with a smile and a wave of his helmet as always as his name was called and he stepped onto the football field. A quick scan later, he'd acknowledged where his family sat with Riley's parents, a few other close family friends…

He did his best to keep himself from sighing. 'Stop it, D. She told you herself that she might be late to the game if traffic was bad. She'll be here.'

Damon joined his teammates in a huddle and shook all other thoughts from his mind. "All right guys," he heard himself saying. "The only thing that matters now is the game. Play hard, do your best. We only have a couple games left together as a team," he eyed Riley and Vin and the other graduating seniors on the team. "Let's make it count!" He stuck a hand into the circle and his teammates followed suit. "Dragons!" he yelled.

"Dragons!!" his team roared back and broke up for the start of the game.

- - -

"Oh my gosh. Could traffic have gone any slower?" Sharon let out sarcastically as she finally parked her car in the crowded parking lot and got out.

Kelly laughed as she quickly joined her best friend's side. "Yes, so be happy. We're here and now both of us can see your man."

"He's not my man," she defended.

"Right, and I'm not a well-known actress or

151

writer or something."

"You're not."

"Not yet anyway," she winked.

Sharon answered with a roll of her eyes. "Come on," she said instead, leading them behind the school. "The field's this way."

"So who is the team playing against tonight?"

"I think a team from a high school about thirty minutes away. I don't think I've seen them play yet."

"What? I thought you've gone to every single game here."

"Not the very first one. I was helping with the house still back then."

"All right. How'd they do then?"

Sharon paused for a brief second. "That's the only game they haven't won this season, now that I think about it."

"They lost?"

"Tied, and the game was a draw because of too many overtimes."

"So you're the lucky charm, huh?"

"Kelly! I go because everyone I know goes to the football games. There's nothing else to do Friday nights."

"Right… It's not like you know the team and the cheer squad," she teased. "Now come on. Let's go in and you can teach me a thing or two about the game."

"What, and not wait until I introduce you to the guys and have them try to explain it to you?"

Kelly snapped her fingers. "Ooh, good one Sharon! I hadn't thought of that idea."

"Me and my big mouth," Sharon groaned as they

rounded the corner and Kelly caught her first glimpse of the game. "Welcome to Dragon territory," she announced dramatically. Even as Kelly hesitated a little bit to take in the sight, Sharon tugged on her arm and dragged her closer. "Come on," she urged as they approached the stands. Sharon paused at the ticket booth and began to take out her wallet.

"You sure you want to show your visitor this game, Sharon? We're not doing so hot tonight."

"Are you serious? But we've been doing so well all semester, Mr. West."

"I know, but the evidence is right there," her government teacher bemoaned as he pointed towards the scoreboard. "It just seems like Damon's just not all together here today."

Sharon couldn't hide the surprised expression on her face. "Is that why you're back here and not on the sidelines?"

"Yeah. I'll go back in a bit, but I just needed a break from this mess. Anyway, why don't you two just go on in," he suggested, waving away Sharon's money. "Maybe your presences will be the luck we need to turn this game around."

Sharon waved bye and thanks to Mr. West and led Kelly in closer to the stands. Before they got too far though, Sharon felt a sharp poke in her side. "What?"

"I told you you're lucky," Kelly teased.

"He said 'us,'" she tossed back as she looked up and scanned the crowd for seats.

"Oh geez," Kelly groaned.

"What now?" Sharon asked, still looking in the

stands.

"Your team's down fourteen points. That person you were talking to wasn't lying."

"Great," Sharon muttered, refusing to look just yet. A second later, she spotted a couple of empty spaces on a bench a few rows up towards the top of the bleachers. She tugged again on Kelly's arm to lead her up to the seats, waving hi to a few people she recognized on the way before sitting down. Only then did she look up at the scoreboard and visibly winced.

"We weren't lying," Kelly repeated, catching Sharon's expression.

"No kidding," she muttered. "Let's just hope a miracle happens in the last quarter or we're beat," she said as the whistle blew, announcing the end of the third quarter. "I wonder what's going on…"

- - -

Damon sighed as the rest of his team trudged back to the bench, not meeting anyone's eyes. As downhearted as his team was, he felt even more so. This team had looked to him for guidance and he had disappointed them all. His plays had been thwarted, his throws had been off – and his heart just wasn't in the game tonight. No one had to say it out loud directly to him, but he could feel everyone blaming him.

'Down by fourteen points… We haven't given up this many points in a game since before I was on this team. We only have a couple more games this season, and every single one counts. Shouldn't that be inspiration enough?"

Damon looked to the stands where his family sat. His parents waved and gave encouraging smiles. Ros and Caleb were both yelling something to him, no doubt trying to lift his spirits as well. He gave a weak wave and then let his eyes wander through the rest of the crowd, taking in the sight in front of him.

A flash of green drew his attention and he turned his head to the left. Ana was rushing over the pick up the pom-pom she had thrown his way. She was looking hard, straight at him and he found himself getting up to come closer.

"What, are you crazy? You're supposed to be cheering!"

She ignored him completely and hissed back at him with a saucy smile. "She's here, Damon, so you better get your act together now that your inspiration is here." Her message delivered, she hurried back over to her squad to cheer alongside them, smoothly getting back into the groove of things.

Damon did not have to think twice about whom Ana had spoken of. He scanned the crowds again, more carefully this time, looking for the face Ana had referred to.

The whistle blew, signaling the imminent start of the fourth quarter. His eyes stayed on the crowd though, trying to find his goal…

And then he locked gazes with Sharon.

In that fraction of a second, everything changed for him. His heart rose even as she smiled and gave him a thumbs up for encouragement. He felt his spirits soar, just knowing she was there giving her support, and the fire that hadn't been there all during the game finally burst into flame. One glance was all it took – even as he moved and bent down to huddle with his teammates, he felt like everything was suddenly clear.

- - -

Riley glanced over at his friend and saw that something was different. He barely listened as Damon gave a quick word of encouragement and called the first play. All he knew was that there was a spark in Damon's eyes and passion back in his voice – Damon was back and confident.

"Let's show them what Dragons are made of," Damon urged as the huddle broke, his teammates fully aware of Damon's transformation and feeding off of the energy.

Riley nodded to himself as he crouched down in position. "This game is about to change…"

22

Sunlight was softly streaming in through Sharon's blinds even as she rolled over and buried herself deeper under her sheets. Kelly blinked her eyes open from where she had slept on the floor and sat up to check on the time.

'Hmm, only 8:15... I guess I can let her sleep a little longer,' she grinned as she settled herself back down comfortably, her mind wide awake, and recalled the events from last night.

A come from behind win for the Dragons had caused the entire home side of the bleachers to pour onto the field to congratulate the team, leaving a stunned opponent to wander off and lick their wounds elsewhere.

Sharon had dragged Kelly onto the field as well, and Kelly had been instantly overwhelmed by the energy of everyone around her. Everyone was hugging and laughing and patting each other on the back... Faces were flying by as Sharon pointed out and introduced people that Kelly had sometimes heard about, but Sharon was relentless in her search for someone in particular...

Ana found them first and immediately drew Sharon close to yell something to her. Whatever Ana had said was lost on the rest of the crowd, but it had made Sharon blush – Kelly found herself liking Ana instantly.

After a quick introduction, Ana led them both by the

hand through the crowd. "How do you know where they are?" Kelly had screamed the question.

Ana turned back with a smile for a second and winked. A short time later, Ana answered the question verbally. "After growing up with these guys, you learn a thing or two about them." The small group left the crowd on the field and approached the bench where a few members of the team were spending time with their families, the crowd respecting their distance.

"Sharon! You made it!"

Kelly watched as a tall, handsome Asian guy ran over and swung Sharon around. Kelly tugged a little on Ana's arm and asked quietly. "That's not Damon, right?" as she looked the guy up and down, trying to remember his name from the pictures Sharon had sent so far.

Kelly caught the look Ana shot her way, but the latter chose to ignore it for the time being. "Right. Kelly, this is Vin. Vin, meet Kelly, one of Sharon's friends."

"It's nice to meet you," he answered. Kelly shook Vin's offered hand, but still kept her thoughts silent, seeing that Vin still had one arm wrapped around Sharon's shoulders. "What did you think? Wasn't that a great game?"

Ana answered for her. "Please! After the way you boys were playing the first three quarters of the game? You guys almost lost it!"

"But we came back and crushed the other guys! Doesn't that count for anything?" Riley asked, joining the group and coming to stand next to Ana.

"Only that you guys got lucky this time," Sharon laughed. "Did you guys really want to give us all heart attacks there? I mean, poor Mr. West!" she kidded.

"Pay no mind to them," Riley said, turning to Kelly.

"The ladies just don't like seeing the fact that guys can be successful too. I'm Riley."

"Kelly," she replied, shaking his hand.

"Ahh, so you're Kelly. Sharon has told us so little about you. Please, enlighten us. Where are you from, how do you know Sharon, and what's Sharon's life story?"

Kelly laughed even as Sharon exclaimed. "Riley! I'd appreciate it if you didn't scare her away just after she's come to visit!"

"Right, as if anyone could be scared by this big teddy bear," Ana smiled, giving her boyfriend a hug.

The chatter continued easily for a couple more minutes until Vin's father called his son away. Kelly then found herself trying to place another voice as it cried out, "Sharon! Sharon!"

A smile broke out on Sharon's face as soon as she heard her name being called and she turned to catch the little girl who was trying to run towards her. The little girl was being held back by another football player, however. The child turned to the guy and tried to swat the hand away that was playfully holding her back. "Damon! Let me go! I just want to say hi to Sharon!"

Kelly immediately looked back up at the guy and tilted her head a little to inspect him closer. The boy was tall... Not as tall as Riley, but definitely a good height for her friend, who was herself 5'6". His black hair was swept back from a pair of bright blue eyes.

'Kind eyes, and warm,' she noted. 'Not hard and cold like Patrick's had been.' She continued with her quick assessment. 'Good build, nice stature, seems like an okay guy so far...'

Then Damon let out a laugh as he finally let his little sister run ahead and Kelly knew instantly what Sharon had seen, what had drawn her best friend to this guy.

'If not for the already high cute factor the boy has, he definitely has heart.'

"And how's the princess doing today?" Sharon asked, holding the girl in her arms.

"Sharon, at the rate you keep calling her princess and treating her like one, she's going to end up believing that she's royalty," Damon joked.

Ros stuck out her tongue at her oldest brother. "I'm okay Sharon. Where were you sitting? I didn't see you when the game started."

"I was a little late. I had to pick up my friend from the airport and there was traffic coming back. Here, say hi to my best friend."

Ros turned in Sharon's arms and waved shyly towards Kelly.

"Shy again Ros? Come on," Damon said as he took his sister from Sharon's arms and carried her himself. "Hi, I'm Damon, this is my little sister Ros, and you must be Kelly. It's a pleasure to finally put a face to your name," he said, shaking Kelly's hand warmly.

"And it's nice to meet you too."

Damon turned back to the girl in his arms. "See? That wasn't so bad was it?" Ros shook her head, grinning. "Then come on, you try."

"No," she grinned.

"No?"

"No."

"I must be mistaken, because I keep hearing a little no, but if I heard that, then I'd have to tickle whoever was saying no, right Sharon?"

"No," she answered back, cheekily.

Damon grinned. "Oh, I'll have to get back to you for

that one. Now Ros, did you say no to me?" Ana rolled her eyes towards Sharon, who just laughed.

"No…"

"What was that?" Damon asked as he started tickling her.

The little girl's laughter rang in the cool evening air as she tried to fight away his hands. "Put me down! Put me down Damon!" Damon willingly obliged after a few more torturous seconds. Again, Ros stuck out her tongue at him. Then she turned to face Kelly. "Hi. My name is Rosaline," she said confidently, sticking out a hand.

Kelly squatted down until she was eye level with the child. "That's a very pretty name, Rosaline. My name is Kelly, and it's very nice to meet you."

"Not like my big brother, huh?" she grinned before darting away to evade Damon's grasp.

"Please forgive her," he said as the group laughed. "She's turning out to be quite a handful."

"Well, you know, little sisters are supposed to look up to their older siblings," Ana joked.

"So that makes me wonder where she got that attitude from…" Riley added.

"Very funny guys. Are we meeting up tonight?"

Kelly gave Sharon a questioning look. "We usually go to the ice-cream parlor after the game to hang out for a bit. Are you up for it?"

"Yeah, come with us," Ana pled. "It'll be fun."

"I'm good to go."

"Great! So we'll see you in a little bit."

"Definitely," Sharon replied.

The two best friends waved bye and headed back to the parking lot, leaving the others behind to grab their stuff from the locker rooms.

A pillow hit Kelly in the face, and she let out a startled yelp. She tossed the pillow right back to Sharon. "What was that for?"

Sharon grinned. "I just wanted to see if you were awake or not.

"Gee, you could have just asked."

"This way was more fun."

"So I can throw a pillow to see if you're awake tomorrow then."

"Nope. My house, my rules."

"But I'm a guest," she retorted.

Sharon answered by tossing the pillow back.

"Ugh, you're so immature!" Kelly laughed as she fell back, hugging the pillow to her.

"And you're not?"

"I am two months older than you."

"And those two months have made all the difference in the world, or so your mom says."

"Hey, leave my mom out of this!"

"She's not in this," Sharon agreed, smiling. "How is she, by the way, and your dad and brother?"

"Oh you know, we're all fine. Just wondering how you're doing is all."

"And what are you going to tell them?"

"That you're definitely a lot happier here than you were those last few months at home. It's almost like you're the person I knew before Patrick was in your life. You're going out, having fun with a great group of people-"

"But certainly not greater than you and Ivana and Jan of course," Sharon interjected.

"Naturally. And don't you ever forget it."

"I wouldn't dare. But still, it is nice. I'm really

lucky to have found a group of people who accept me for who I am."

"Do they know about Patrick?"

Sharon shook her head.

"I think you should tell them," Kelly said. "It would be good for you."

"Oh yeah? And how do you figure that one?"

"Sharon, I can't be here all the time for you, like it or not, and neither can the girls back home. I just think it would be a good idea if some other people knew, people who weren't directly involved. They might have other insight on the whole ordeal."

"What else is there to know?" Sharon found herself spitting out. "I was in an abusive relationship with a guy, and it got more than a little ugly. Thankfully, things stopped before they could get any uglier. End of story. I don't need more people to tell me I screwed up by going on with that relationship, thinking that I could fix things if I had tried just a little harder or held on just a little bit longer."

Her best friend sat up so they were more at eye level. "Sharon, I'm not telling you to write your autobiography here and hand a copy out to everyone new who comes into your life." Kelly continued, gently now. "All I'm saying is just think about it. And if this group of people is as great as I think they are, I doubt they'll hold your past against you."

"I know, I know. I just… It's just hard enough thinking about it. I'm at the point where I'm finally not thinking about Patrick each time I go to bed or wake up in the middle of the night with the thought that he's found me and he's lurking somewhere nearby. I'd like to keep it that way."

"Talk to Ana. See what she thinks and go from there."

From where she lay in bed, Sharon just nodded and hoped that in bringing up her past, she wouldn't be welcoming back the nightmares at the same time.

23

"How could you not notice!?" Kelly was screeching as the two best friends walked through the streets later that afternoon.

"Can you yell this out any louder and just let the whole world know?"

"I definitely could do that, but then you'd kick me out of your house."

Sharon laughed. "That's probably true, but still! You're telling me that in those couple minutes after the game yesterday, you're 100% sure that I have not one but two guys wrapped around my fingers?"

"Well, in the first couple of minutes, I definitely wasn't imagining Vin draped across your shoulders."

"He was just being friendly," Sharon retorted, but a faint blush appeared on her face anyway.

"And what is this?! This is the second time I've seen you blush in less than twenty-four hours! I swear, this is not like you," Kelly was laughing.

"Last night was nothing. I was just excited."

"Sharon, you're such a bad liar! What did Ana say to you?"

"Nothing…" she tried.

"And again, you're lying! Come on and just tell me!"

"You'll laugh and hold it against me."

"It concerns the guys, doesn't it?"

"Well it's definitely about the other guy you think is wrapped around my finger."

"What about Damon?"

"Hush, Kelly! This is a small town I live in!"

"Then fess up and just tell me already!"

"She asked how it felt to be the reason why the game turned around."

"A-ha! I told you he likes you! He was obviously thrown off without you around."

"And the weight of someone relying on you like that is a good thing?"

"Oh don't be so serious! Isn't it enough that he's interested?"

"I hardly call this interest. It sounds a little more like dependency."

'Shar, just stop it!" Kelly laughed. "You are head over heels for Damon and don't even deny it. I saw the way you two were last night."

"And what way would that be? We never got close together once!"

"Um, I don't think I imagined that hug between you two before we left!"

"Well, besides that then, which wasn't anything besides friendly. What else was there?" she challenged.

"The connection was in your eyes," she announced with dramatic flair. "The way you looked at him, the way he looked at you, the way you two would look at each other without the other person noticing, and neither of you noticing me watching both of you and me thinking to myself, 'gosh, will they just get this over with and do something?'"

Sharon burst out laughing. "Kelly, you are just

too much sometimes."

Her best friend just groaned. "You're not listening to me! Here," she said, pulling out her cell phone. "Call him and ask him if he wants to hang out."

Sharon just gawked at her. "I can't do that."

"And why not?"

"Because… because, you're here and I just can't!" she sputtered.

"And that's your reason? I'm a big girl. I can take care of myself for a couple hours while you're out. Just face the facts that he likes you. I can see it!"

"You're biased – you're my best friend."

"If you can't take my word for it, tell me what in the world would so that you'd finally believe me?"

"It just has to be more obvious is all."

"Obvious? Fine. I'll just put mirrors all around your head so you can keep an eye on the boy yourself and catch him when he gives you those longing looks I'm telling you he gives."

"Eww!" Sharon exclaimed, trying not to laugh at the mental image she was getting. "Now you're making me sound like I'm the dependent one."

"Aren't you?" came the cheeky reply.

"Oh shut up," Sharon laughed as the two ducked into a little shop to grab a bite to eat.

- - -

The clock chiming 12:30 and Damon's stomach growling signaled the end of their morning study session. "I'm hungry," Damon announced, pushing himself from the table and leaning back in his chair.

"No kidding," Ana replied, not bothering to look up from what she was writing yet. "Your stomach has been grumbling since you got here. Didn't you have breakfast?"

"I woke up late so no. I had time to brush my teeth and grab my backpack before coming over."

"Well, at least you brushed your teeth. You know, you could have just called to let me know you were running behind."

"And miss out on my full daily, recommended dose of Ana time? I would rather die."

"Oh please. The last thing I need on my head right now is to be the cause of your death."

"Ahh, but you will be one day. You do keep threatening to kill me."

"One privilege of being best friends. I do get the honor if ever you do overstep your boundaries," she said as she finally pushed herself back from the table to look over at him.

"I'll keep that in mind," Damon smirked.

Ana got up and walked to the refrigerator. "You're okay for leftovers, right?"

"Another highlight of my week. You know I love your mom's cooking."

"And the truth is out. That's the only reason why you're even here, huh? We could have been studying at the library, you know."

"And have my grumbling stomach annoy everyone in a ten-foot radius? Thanks, but I think I'll pass on the dirty looks of death."

Ana laughed. "It'd serve you right! You should have gone to bed earlier and eaten breakfast before you got here."

"Oh come on! Don't I get any reward for pulling the game around last night?"

"What other reward do you need from me? Your girl showed up to both the game AND to Marty's shop to hang out afterwards." She paused, smirking as Damon began to blush. "And... I do believe I caught a hug between you two before she and Kelly had to leave last night."

Damon's blush intensified at Ana's last comment. "It was nothing."

Ana laughed. "Don't lie to me Damon. If anything else, we both know that the person we should be thanking for turning last night's game around was a certain female who is not in this room. The only question left to ask is when are you finally going to ask the girl out on a date?" She placed a plate of food in front of her friend and sat back down.

"You make it sound like it's so easy but it's not! You're lucky you already have someone like Riley around."

"And I just want to make sure that you find the same kind of happiness. I know I'm lucky, and I'm grateful for it, but that doesn't stop me from worrying about you too sometimes. Besides, you should be glad I actually like Sharon. She's a good girl and I think she'd be great for you. When are you going to ask her out?"

He sighed. "Not anytime soon. I saw that Vin was pretty close with her last night."

"You saw that, huh?"

"It was a little hard to miss," he replied quietly. "I can't just ignore Vin's feelings like that. He's a good friend too Ana, and I don't want to jeopardize that either."

The two ate their meals in silence for a little while before Ana put a voice to the thoughts going on in her head. "You know, we should find Vin a girlfriend."

"And do you have someone in mind? You know none of the girls here are worth it."

"I don't know. What about Linda?"

"There's no Linda in our class."

"I know. I was talking about junior pres Linda."

Damon stared off for a moment as he chewed his food. "It wouldn't be a bad match, I'll be honest. I guess it just doesn't help that Vin can be a little picky sometimes."

"And with good reason. But, if you're not opposed to letting me try my magic…"

"What is going on in that head of yours, Ana?"

"Nothing besides inviting a few more people to help out with the pre-Thanksgiving feast… And looking at the serving arrangement once more…"

"As long as it's not obvious," he replied with a shake of his head but a hopeful glimmer in his eyes.

Ana nodded. "Not obvious," she repeated, agreeing. "Besides, we needed a few more people to help out anyway," she added with a grin, her mind already racing with all the possibilities.

"Riley's really lucky to have you, you know that?"

She shrugged. "What's even better is he knows it too. Don't worry Damon. You'll win the girl yet."

"I hope so…"

24

Sharon entered the cafeteria and dropped her backpack off in one corner along with everyone else's. "All right, I'm here. Point me in my direction."

"Hi, Sharon. Let me see where you are…" Mrs. Faulkin flipped through a couple of pages on her clipboard. "I think you're over with Ana at the salad… Oh wait. I forgot that the arrangements changed. You're with Damon at mashed potatoes."

Sharon suppressed the tingling she got in her spine at the news, but couldn't hide the smile as she approached the table where Damon was standing and talking to another class board member. She came to a stop next to Damon and listened in on the conversation…

Or at least tried to listen until Damon shifted his weight and casually wrapped his left arm around her shoulders. The act had been innocent enough, but the action had immediately sent a warm feeling rushing through her body.

Damon finished his conversation with a member of the sophomore student council before he turned to Sharon, enjoying the feel of the girl in his arms. "So my dear, are you ready to spend the next hour working with me?"

"Somehow, even though spooning mashed potatoes isn't normally my idea of fun, I guess I can tolerate it with you around," she answered with a grin.

He smiled back and gave her a quick squeeze before letting her go. As reluctant as he had been, a motion out of the corner of his eye let him know that he'd let go not a moment too soon. Vin had just arrived and was on his way over to talk to Mrs. Faulkin. He wasn't sure what Ana had in mind for their friend, but he figured it would be best not to try and jeopardize anything just then.

Sharon took a deep breath in hopes of calming her racing heart, but it wasn't helping that Damon was still standing right next to her and her skin was still tingling from his touch. 'Kelly's going to kill herself for missing that! I can just see her screaming later when I tell her. Then again, she'll probably kill me for not doing anything more about it too. Oh Kelly…'

A small chuckle escaped her and Damon was quick to notice. "What's so funny?"

"Oh, I was just thinking about something."

"Me?"

Sharon's jaw dropped open for a moment as she stared at Damon before she started laughing. "What makes you think you're so funny?" she laughed.

"Aren't I?" he asked, but he was laughing along with her anyway.

"If you must know," she continued after she got her breath back. "I was really thinking about Kelly," she replied, telling herself she was telling the truth, if not the complete truth.

"Ahh, I see. She's coming to the feast, right?"

"She wouldn't miss it for the world."

"Good, because she'd be missing out on some serious mashed potatoes otherwise."

"Oh, like you slaved over the stove all day to make these," she retorted sarcastically.

"I was in class same as you so no, unfortunately. But she would still be missing out on our wonderful service."

"Because it's so hard to scoop the potatoes onto a plate?"

He found himself laughing again. "You know, you're just asking for trouble Sharon. I don't think I've ever gotten this much sarcasm from you before."

"You have a point there. I guess that means I'm getting very comfortable around you," she said with a shrug.

"And is that a good thing?"

"That depends."

"On what?"

"Do you want me to stop?"

Damon hesitated only a little bit before answering. "Never. It makes me like you even more."

This time, Sharon was sure he could hear the beating of her heart and felt her face flush. 'Did I just hear what I think he said? Surely, he didn't mean it the way I think he does, or does he?' she asked herself in her mind even as she spoke. "And is that a good thing?"

"That depends," Damon found himself echoing their earlier conversation.

"On what?"

"Do you want me to stop?" Despite the innocent

tone with which he'd asked the question, there was a mischievous twinkle in his eyes – blue eyes that Sharon knew she could easily lose herself in if she gave herself the chance.

Sharon opened her mouth but found no words coming out. Her heart was hammering in her chest telling her to say no for fear of rejection, but at the same time, her mind was screaming to finally admit out loud to the person she liked that yes, she did like him as more than a friend. 'Strange,' she let herself dwell vaguely. 'My mind's telling me to go with my emotions, but my heart is so scared of following through…'

Thankfully, she did not need to reply. Mrs. Faulkin chose that moment to clap her hands to get everyone's attention. "All right, all right everyone. Listen up." Sharon turned away from Damon's expectant gaze and tried to clear her mind. Once she was satisfied she had everyone's attention, Mrs. Faulkin went on. "I just want to thank you all again for helping out today. It may not seem like it, but we really do appreciate what you're doing. You are all helping to maintain the strong bond between this school and the rest of the community." She continued to give a bit of the history of the school feed before pausing, taking a little break to smile proudly at all the student volunteers in the room. "Anyway, doors open in just a few minutes. Make sure you have your gloves on and have fun!"

With that, Mrs. Faulkin gave a final smile and headed towards the doors to make sure everything was all set to go there.

"Gloves, milady?" Damon asked, holding a pair

of the thin plastic gloves towards Sharon.

She wrinkled her nose but accepted the pair anyway. "You'd think they'd make these just a little bit smaller to fit real people's hands, wouldn't you?"

"But then I couldn't make fun of how small your hands look in them," he teased.

"Be nice. We're going to be stuck together for at least the next hour."

"And I'm looking forward to every second of it," he smiled.

"So you can make fun of me the entire time?"

"That's only part of it. I just like being around you."

"Well, I guess there's nothing wrong with that," she answered back slowly.

"There better not be because I intend to do it more."

"I think I can handle that," she grinned.

"Good, because I like you, Sharon."

Once more, Sharon could not stop the fierce blush that came unbeckoned onto her face. She mumbled something unintelligible, but Damon knew better than to push his luck just then. It was enough that what he'd been meaning to say was now out there, and he did not regret it one bit. 'She won't be telling the whole world, and at least Ana will be off my back now too.'

From a few tables down, Ana was giving Damon a look. Once she'd caught his eye, she nodded her head over towards Sharon, whose face was still bright red. He just smiled and shrugged. She gave him a quick smirk before turning back to the girl next to her.

Damon grinned to himself as he put on a pair of the plastic gloves and grabbed a serving spoon. 'This is going to be one interesting day...' he thought to himself as he watched Mrs. Faulkin prepare to open the doors.

- - -

Sharon rolled her shoulders back and stretched her neck. After more than an hour of spooning potatoes, she was getting a little tired of standing on her feet.

"You want to take a quick break? I can cover for a couple of minutes if you want to get some fresh air," Damon offered.

"Only if you don't mind."

"Not at all. Most everyone is eating at the moment. I can serve for a few minutes. Just don't stay out too long – it's cold out there."

"Thanks Damon. I owe you one."

He smiled and shrugged it off before shooing her away.

She left him behind and dropped off the gloves in a trash can on her way out. She braced herself for the cold before pushing the doors open and walking outside. A brisk wind was blowing, and Sharon was thankful that she'd kept her sweatshirt tied around her waist. She pulled it up over her head and drew it on, thankful for her arms being covered and for being able to breathe in some fresh air.

The past hour had been a great one. She and Damon had just used the time in between people to chat and laugh and just hang out. His family had said hi when they had come in, Ros proudly wearing the pilgrim hat she'd cut out from school. Kari had, as always, ignored Sharon and did her sweet-talking to Damon before moving on to eat with a bunch of the other cheerleaders at the other side of the gym. Her parents hadn't shown up yet with Kelly, but a glance at her watch let her know that they'd be coming in any minute now.

One more turn around the front door and sure enough, she heard familiar faces calling out her name.

Sharon smiled and walked a little bit towards the parking lot to join her parents and Kelly as they walked up.

"Are you crazy Sharon, staying outside like this? It's freezing out here!" Kelly exclaimed, her breath coming out in puffy clouds as she spoke.

"And it was getting stuffy inside. I needed the fresh air."

"Did you eat yet?" her mother asked, coming up.

"Not yet. I wasn't really hungry inside."

"Damon distracting you?"

"Hush, Kelly! I'm on school grounds, and I don't know who's around to hear."

Her best friend smirked as they opened the doors and a wall of warm air and tantalizing smells greeted them. "I'll take that as a yes," she replied even as Sharon rolled her eyes.

"The food line starts right here," she ended up pointing. "Just grab a plate, fill it up with whatever you want, and find a place to sit. I'll find you guys when I'm done, okay?"

Her parents and Kelly agreed and began their

trek around all the food stations after paying for their meals. She herself went straight back to the mashed potatoes and took the fresh pair of gloves that Damon was holding out towards her as she came back. "Thanks."

"You're welcome. I see you found some people."

"What can I say? I have perfect timing."

"Yeah right! If I remember correctly, I was the one who told you to take a break in the first place."

"But I could have refused you so there."

"You're not going to refuse when you're tired."

"Are you telling me I looked like crap?"

"Wait, what? How did you come up with that one?" he laughed.

"You haven't heard that that's usually a guy's way of saying that a girl isn't looking too good?"

"No!" he denied, still laughing

"But it makes sense."

"I was just commenting!"

"Yeah right," Sharon grinned back. "I see what you really think of me now."

"You have no idea!" he laughed.

"Then tell me!"

"What do you mean you have no idea? I already told you," he smiled.

"And that could mean anything," she replied back easily.

"You better tone it down you two lovebirds. Aren't you guys supposed to be working?"

Kelly's remark produced its desired effect on her best friend, who felt some blood rush to her face.

"It's nice to see you too, Kelly," Damon smiled. "How's the vacation treating you?"

"Great food, great company, no teachers on my back about homework – I'm not complaining."

"And what about you Damon?" Sharon's father asked. "How are you these days?"

"I'm not injured and I'm not failing my classes, so I guess I'm doing pretty well actually."

"That's good to hear. Are you two done soon?"

Even as Sharon shrugged, Damon replied that they'd find them as soon as they were able. "It should only be a little while longer before it turns into a self-serve buffet," he added.

Soon after he had said those words, Mrs. Faulkin announced to the volunteers that they were being relieved and it was their turn to eat.

Despite the gym being pretty full of people already eating their fill, there was still plenty of food for the volunteers to eat and Sharon and Damon each piled their plates high with food before meandering their ways over to their own families. Sharon took a seat next to Kelly and easily entered in on the conversation her family was having with Marty, who had come down for the feast, while a couple of tables down, Damon and Ana took seats at the table their families were sharing.

"You told her, huh?" Ana found herself asking Damon quietly as everyone around them continued to talk. Damon just nodded and left it at that. Ana smiled and nodded back a little, her mind already working at how else she could help to bring Sharon and Damon closer together.

25

"Sharon?" Kelly asked sleepily from the floor. Sharon was tossing and turning in bed, mumbling under her breath all the while. When she realized she was not going to get any response from her friend, she got up. "Sharon?" she asked again, coming closer.

"Go away," she heard Sharon mutter. "Please, just go away."

"Sharon, it's me."

"No, please. Don't. You'll hurt me again," she was whimpered.

Kelly's heart broke, understanding the nightmare Sharon was reliving the more she listened, and herself unsure if she should wake her friend up or let her ride out the nightmare in hopes of not remembering it in the morning. As Sharon's movements became more frantic though, Kelly couldn't take it anymore. "Come on Sharon," she said gently, reaching out and starting to shake her awake. "It's just a dream."

Sharon tried to push her away. "Go away. Stay away from me," desperation sounding in her words.

Kelly just tried all the harder until finally, Sharon sat up with her eyes wide open. Immediately, she let her friend go but sat back on the bed. "You with me Sharon?"

Sharon blinked a few times and looked around

her quickly, trying to orient herself. It was still night, but her heart was racing and her skin felt flushed. She looked back at Kelly and nodded a little bit, unable to say anything as realization slowly hit her. She closed her eyes again and tried to stifle the sobs that were coming. She felt Kelly come close and felt herself being enveloped in her friend's arms.

"It's okay, Sharon. It's okay now," she heard Kelly whisper over and over. "He's not here and he can't hurt you anymore. It's okay."

It was a long time before either could sleep again that night.

- - -

Sharon sighed. "The thing is, I thought I was getting over it all and now this."

"Stop it Sharon," Kelly said as they walked through downtown on their way to the library later that afternoon. The two had finally fallen asleep again just as the sky was lightening and so had slept in until noon. Now, the two walked to meet with Sharon's friends at the library for a group study session. "You can't go on kicking yourself like this. How do you think it makes me feel knowing that I have to leave tomorrow and you're all down and out of it like this?"

"I know, I know, and I'm sorry Kelly. I don't mean to be all out of it. I'm just… I want to tell myself it's really all over and actually believe it. I just don't want to deal with this anymore."

Kelly nodded, but before she could add any more input, they heard a female voice call out to them.

Sharon and Kelly turned and watched as Ana approached. "Hey guys! How have the past couple of days been for you?"

"It was nice," Kelly answered for them. "Lots of good food on Thanksgiving, plenty of shopping yesterday…"

"Oh yeah? That's good! Where'd you guys go?"

"We actually drove out to the mall that you mentioned I should go try," Sharon answered. "You're right Ana, the place is huge!"

"I figured it'd be a good place for you to go when you miss more of the brand name stuff and just want to get away from the local stores."

"But the local stores are so cute too," Kelly added. "I just wish I had more room in my suitcase for everything I wish I could have gotten."

"Don't worry. You know I'll end up sending a lot of stuff up to you anyway," Sharon laughed a little.

"This is true," Kelly smiled.

"It's so sad that you have to leave so soon. When's your flight out again?"

"Tomorrow morning."

"Gotcha."

The three girls continued to walk their way closer to the library a little bit longer before Ana noticed the tired look in Sharon's eyes. "Sharon, are you all right? Don't take this the wrong way, but you look a little tired," concern filling her voice. She didn't miss the quick look Sharon and Kelly shared.

Sharon shrugged a little. "I had a nightmare last night. I couldn't sleep for a while after that is all."

Ana wasn't convinced. "Are you sure?"

Again, Kelly and Sharon shared a glance, Kelly

indicating that it was up to Sharon if she was going to tell her story or not. They stopped walking and Sharon looked up at the library that suddenly stood before them, seemingly connecting her thoughts and debating whether this was the way to do what needed to be done and say what needed to be said. "Ana, I'm going to tell you something that I don't want anyone else to know."

She nodded. "You have my word."

Sharon nodded as well and indicated that they take a seat on a bench near the front of the library. Then she told her story.

- - -

"There you guys are. We were getting a little worried," Riley said as he stood up from the table to hug Ana. "I was beginning to worry that this may be the first time ever Ana hasn't shown up for a study session."

"Keep that up and you're on your own next semester in Gietzen's class," she threw back with a gleam in her eye, hugging back and taking the seat next to him at the table. "Sorry we're late. We lost track of time," she whispered as she, Kelly, and Sharon took the other three seats at the table.

"Not a problem at all, although the motivation to study was not that great without you lording over us to study," Damon teased. Ana just stuck out her tongue at Damon and pulled out some books from her backpack. "Kelly, Sharon, I trust you both are doing well."

"Just perfect," Sharon answered cheerily with a

smile.

Damon was keen enough to notice, however, that the smile she gave did not quite reach her eyes. He looked over towards Kelly and Ana, but both quickly avoided his eyes. 'All right... What was that about?'

"Perfect enough that we're all stuck in here in the library during vacation?" Riley was grinning, oblivious to what had just occurred.

"Be quiet, Riley," Ana whispered, rolling her eyes. "I'd hardly call this a vacation with finals coming up."

"Does it always have to be about school?" Riley asked, but was answered with a sharp "Shh!" from Kelly, who grinned at the boy before curling up in her seat and pulling one of her own books close to start reading. "Outnumbered by the girls," Riley groaned quietly to Damon even as his friend grinned and looked down at a notebook and settled in for some quality study time.

- - -

A jab in the ribs brought Damon out of his nap a while later. He jerked himself upright to find his friends grinning at him. He rubbed his side a little and scowled a bit at Riley, but a gentle hand on his arm stopped him from saying anything.

"Pack up, Damon. I think we're going to call it a night and grab some food."

A quick glance at his watch and he nodded at Sharon's words, flipping his notebook closed. After stuffing that away in his messenger bag, he stood up to stretch before joining everyone on the trek outside.

The troupe found that the sun had just set and a chilling wind had picked up. Ana instinctively found her way closer into her boyfriend's arms. Kelly was fine in her coat, but Sharon was not doing so well, the change of weather catching her unaware.

"I told you that it was going to get cold," Kelly stated the obvious as they started walking towards downtown. "And your mom's going to kill me now since you're going to get sick."

"Oh quiet. I'm not going to get sick."

"Still, you better put this on," Damon said, already wrapping his jacket around her shoulders.

"Not you too! What about you? You have no jacket now and your parents will kill me if you get sick before the big game!"

"I won't get sick." She gave him a pointed look even as she tried to shrug herself out of the jacket. "I insist, Sharon," he said, his hands coming down on her shoulders and effectively clamping the jacket down on her. "We need you to stay warm."

Sharon bit her tongue from arguing back, seeing how pointless it was going to be, and admitted defeat. "Thanks, Damon," she said instead and wrapped the jacket closer around her to regain some lost heat.

"You're welcome. Besides, it looks good on you."

She just rolled her eyes. "Now you're kidding me. I'm swimming in this thing!"

He just shook his head and continued smiling as the group walked onwards to dinner.

26

The bell rang and Damon joined his classmates in exiting the gym. Their first week back after the Thanksgiving holiday was quickly coming to a close and already, a winter vibe was in the air. His breath came out in small clouds of air as he moved towards the main building, where he quickly scanned the halls for his friends and spotted Sharon heading towards her locker. He braced himself and took a step in her direction. Before he could take another though, he felt an arm link with his and steer him the opposite way. Startled, he looked down found himself looking into Kari's face. "Kari, hi! What's up?"

"Oh, you know. Not much. I was wondering what you were doing after the game on tomorrow."

"I'm probably just going to Marty's and hang out with everyone else, why?"

"Oh, come on, Damon! It's the big game! That's not enough!"

He couldn't help but give her a look. "What's not great about spending time with my friends and family? You know they're important to me."

"Oh, I know that," she said, brushing his comment away with a wave of her hand and not understanding truly what that meant to him. "But I thought you'd want to do something else for a change."

"And you have a suggestion." Damon wasn't really asking.

A sparkle came into her eyes as she flashed him a dazzling smile. "Well, now that you mention it, I was thinking that we could go to the city and celebrate."

"The city? It's almost an hour away! I'll be too tired to party by the time we get there."

"Oh come on! It'll be fun!"

"Sorry, Kari. I don't think I can do it," he said, disengaging his arm from hers and stepping away. "Besides, I don't know if anyone else would want to go."

"No one else has to go. It'd just be you and me."

Damon raised an eyebrow with that comment but politely shook his head. "Sorry. Anyway, I better get going. I'll see you later though, okay?" He gave a half-hearted smile and turned to go back in the other direction. A quick scan down the hall, however, showed him that Sharon was already gone from her locker and nowhere in sight. He sighed and started to walk to his next class, oblivious to the stormy look on Kari's face for just having been brushed off.

The next hour sped by for Sharon as she worked on her English exam. A glance at the clock let her know that she was making pretty good time, so she sat back in her seat and closed her eyes for a moment. She took in a few breaths and rolled her head a little bit before sitting forward again to continue her essay.

When the bell rang twenty minutes later, she quickly grabbed her stuff and joined the crowd leaving the classroom. "What'd you think of that one?"

Sharon turned toward her classmate and smiled. "Well, it wasn't my worst timed-write ever, I can tell you that, but neither was it my best. What do you think Andrea?"

"I don't know, really. What I do know is that my hand hurts from all that writing and I think I am officially tired of poetry."

Sharon laughed in agreement. "Too true. I don't think I could take any more of "The Dawn" or anything like it. How sad, I think I'm almost looking forward to starting plays next semester."

"Sharon! Just the person I wanted to see!"

She felt her heart skip a beat as an arm wrapped around her shoulders. "Hey Damon, what's up?"

"I want to talk to you. Is now a good time?"

"Sure. I'll see you later Andrea, all right?" She waved bye and let herself be led to their next destination.

"Do you need anything from your locker?" he asked her.

"Nope. I'll just grab my stuff after lunch."

"Okay. Would you mind if I grab my stuff first then?"

"Not at all," she smiled and headed a little further down the hall. "So what do you want to talk to me about?"

"Well, I was just wondering," he started slowly, suddenly unsure of himself. He'd been steeling himself for this moment for so long now, he suddenly didn't know what to say.

"Yes?" she prompted, still smiling. They had

reached his locker and he looked to be devoting an unusual amount of concentration towards undoing his lock. "Is everything all right?" She placed a hand on his arm in what she hoped was a comforting gesture.

"Yeah, sure, fine," he answered quickly, finally getting the combination right and trying to calm his racing heart down. "Look, Sharon, I was just wondering if you'd like to go to winter ball with me."

Time stood still for a moment as his question registered in her mind. "Are you serious?"

He nodded, trying to read the expression on her face.

"Oh Damon, I'd love to go with you," she broke out into a smile. "But I can't."

One moment, his heart had been soaring and he had felt on top of the world. Then the last part of her sentence hit him, dropping him back down to earth with a sudden jolt and leaving him suddenly feeling a little sick. "Oh." Damon suddenly found the inside of his locker to be quite interesting.

"Damon, it's not you."

"Right…" he said, not quite believing her and still not quite sure what had just happened.

After she realized he wasn't going to say anything more, she tried again, wanting to make him understand. "Really Da-"

"Did Vin ask you already?" he found himself interrupting her and asking before he could stop himself.

"Huh? Vin? No, he didn't." A puzzled look settled on her face. "Why?"

"Well, he asked you for homecoming, didn't he? And you said yes to him then."

"Yeah, but he didn't ask me this time. Didn't you hear? He's already asked one of the sophomores and they're going to go together."

"No, I hadn't heard." He looked genuinely surprised and smiled for a brief moment as he thought about congratulating Ana for her work before frowning again. "Then who else asked you to go to the ball with them?"

"No one else asked me. Just you. I'm actually flattered you asked."

"Then why won't you go with me?" He couldn't help the little bit of whining that came with that last question.

She smiled but didn't find it in her heart to tease at that moment. "Because I'm supposed to be boarding a plane right around the time the dance is supposed to start."

"Plane?"

"Yeah, a plane. You know, it's a big type of machine that flies people through the skies-"

"Very funny, Sharon. I know what a plane is."

She chuckled. "Yeah, all right. Anyway, the dance is the day after we get out for winter break, right?"

"Yeah…"

"So yeah, I can't make it. It's tradition for my family to go skiing with Kelly and her family over winter break. We made these plans months ago, before I knew there was going to be a dance that night."

It took a few moments, but as soon as he was

able to understand what she had just revealed to him, relief visibly came across Damon's features and she found herself smiling with him.

"If it helps any," she continued, letting herself be bold and linking her arm through his as they turned to walk out to lunch. "I would have said yes."

"Really?"

"Of course. Is mine a face that would lie to you?"

"I sure hope not."

She laughed. "Thanks for the vote of confidence! I suppose I should work on my poker face then."

"Except we've already established you suck at cards so that's not going to happen," he teased.

They were still teasing each other when they approached their usual lunch table. Ana shot him with an inquisitive glance at Sharon's arm, which was still linked with his, but he just smiled and shrugged, thankful that Sharon hadn't noticed the interchange. 'Nothing can bring me down from feeling as happy as I feel right now with Sharon here at my side,' he thought. Damon glanced over at Sharon, who was still beaming. 'Nope. Absolutely nothing.'

27

Damon grunted as a formidable player rushed at him and sent the two of them off of their feet. A second later, he felt what little air left in his lungs leave on impact with the frozen turf underneath him. 'Well that's not good,' he thought to himself.

A roar of outrage bellowed from the bleachers on his right while cheers issued from the stands to his left. He felt the body on top of his immediately get off and a hand reached back down to help pull Damon up. "Good play," he puffed, thanking the opposing player.

"I gotta keep you on your toes, right?" the other guy winked before jogging back to the rest of his team.

"Brett! Riley! What's going on? Where was the defense on Damon? Get it together you two and guard him!" he could hear Coach West's voice cutting through the clamor even as Damon motioned in what he hoped was a reassuring way that he was okay. He met his teammates in another huddle, but before he could call out the next play, Riley questioned, "You okay Damon?"

"Fine. Don't worry about me."

"We're your defense, D. That's our job," another teammate cracked.

He looked over at Brett and the rest of his team. "Then you better get to it before Coach has a heart attack, all right?" he smirked. "Okay. Four minutes left of the first quarter of our big championship game and we're still on our side of the field. Let's see if we can up the tempo to this game a bit. Vin, are you good for the 'First Play'?"

"Ready when you are."

Damon nodded. "All right. Let's see if we can't put up the first points. 'Big Play One.' Go Dragons," he yelled, sticking a fist into the center of the huddle.

"Dragons!" the rest of the team cried as they added their hands to Damon's before breaking the huddle and reforming the offensive line.

Damon stole a glance over toward the stands on his right and easily found his family from within the crowd and then spotted Sharon sitting with her parents a little ways away. Seeing that she had caught his eye, she quickly gave him a gloved two thumbs up and yelled some support that he couldn't hear, but he grinned back nonetheless, his heart racing for a moment from more than the adrenaline of the game.

He turned back to the scene in front of him on the field, took a breath, and without warning to the other side, called the next play. The ball sailed smoothly into his hands and he set off running to his left. The opposing team pursued him, falling for the ruse, and for this, he was thankful. Just as it looked like he'd be rushing the ball forward himself, he suddenly threw the ball hard to the right side of the field and watched it spiral perfectly right into the arms of an unguarded Vin.

His friend didn't really need to hear the

encouragement Damon was yelling, but he yelled it all the same. He was so intent on watching the play progress, he didn't see the flash of brown and gold rushing towards him until just the moment before impact. He gave another grunt as his feet lost contact with the ground before finding himself back on his back for the second time in less than five minutes, the whistle blowing shrilly a few seconds later and the flag being thrown.

The field was awash in noise as Damon picked himself up off the ground, not missing the menacing look his latest tackler had in his eyes. He glanced over at Coach West and saw him practically jumping up and down screaming at one of the other referees about the blatant tackle. "Don't you have eyes ref? That was a clear attack on one of my players!"

A glance over at the other side of the field showed the Diamondbacks' coach looking unconcerned by his player's actions. The two caught glances and Damon couldn't help but frown a little from inside his helmet. 'Well that certainly changes things,' he thought to himself as he made his way over toward the rest of the team.

"D, you okay?" Vin asked, panting a little as he rejoined his teammates.

"Fine," he answered, thankful for the bulky padding he was wearing. "How far did you get?"

"I think just shy of their 30-yard line, but I'm not quite sure."

"That's good enough for a first down. Listen, I think the other team's gonna pick it up from here on in though."

"Why do you think that?" a player asked from his right.

"Their coach," he said simply, the grim tone of his voice indicating his certainty on the matter.

"So what are we playing next then?"

"'All Out.' We're running plays 17, 21, and 6."

"Serious? We have three quarters still to go!"

Damon nodded. "And I want to get us up on that board with as much of a cushion as possible before they get their hands on the ball."

His team agreed and broke up the huddle. With less than two minutes left in the quarter, Damon led the offense in a couple of quick succession plays to get them successfully into the end zone, much to the delight of his team and fans while leaving the Diamondback supporters to boo and hiss. A glance towards his coach let him know that he was sending in their kicker to finish off the job rather than risk an extra play. He nodded to let Coach West know he understood and started jogging back towards the bleachers, slapping his teammate on the back as the two passed each other. "Good luck out there Louis," he called.

"I'll be back in a few," his teammate called back as he moved forward to attempt the extra point.

Seconds later, a roar came from behind Damon as another point was added to their score. Damon glanced over at the other side and saw that, rather than screaming up a storm, however, the Diamondback coach seemed to be contemplating something, his face almost unreadable. "Coach West," he said, gaining his attention.

Mr. West followed Damon's gaze. "I know. He's

trying to come up with a way to get back into the game, so he's going to play that team different come next quarter. Just watch your back, okay? I wouldn't put it past them to try something a little bit more than an uncalled for tackle next time."

Damon nodded in understanding and moved off to get a drink. He gave Ana a wink as she led her group through another cheer before settling down on a seat and forcing himself to relax for a few moments while the defensive line got started on the field at the turn of the quarter. A minute later, he felt a small pair of arms hug him from behind. "Hi Damon!"

"Ros, hey!" he smiled, turning around and pulling his sister up onto the bench next to him. "What are you doing down here?"

"I wanted to get some candy with Sharon. See?" she showed him the box of chocolates that she was holding in one hand. "Do you want some?"

"No thanks, but thank you. And you don't go eating it all at once either, okay?"

"Okay. I love you."

"I love you too," he smiled. "Go on now, okay?"

The little girl nodded, giving her big brother one last hug before sliding off the bench and running over to grab Sharon's hand. "Good luck Damon, and be careful out there," he heard Sharon say.

"Thanks," he grinned and watched as Sharon and Ros carefully walked back up the bleachers hand in hand. His gaze lingered on them for a little bit longer before a chuckle next to him made him turn around. "What?"

Riley grinned innocently. "You're hopeless, you

know that right?"

"Oh shut up."

Riley laughed. "Seriously man, I can't believe you're waiting this long to break the question to her."

"I've waited this long, it can wait until the end of the game."

"All right. The guys and I will try to make sure you don't get too roughed up then," he chuckled as the two stood up. "We gotta make sure you look presentable to your lady love after the game."

Damon punched his friend lightly on the arm as they walked back onto the field. "Be careful out there!" they heard Coach West yell out to them. The defensive line leaving the field gave similar sentiments, and Damon mentally prepared himself for the coming battle.

"All right. We're still up by seven points. Let's see if we can't keep these Diamondbacks at bay. Let's run the Fire Sequence, all right?"

"Dragons!" erupted from the group as once more, the team got into position for another play.

Both teams scored in the next forty-five minutes, and despite the game winding down into the last ten minutes of the third quarter, neither side seemed to be willing to let up. A look at Sharon's face and the faces of his family in the crowds visibly showed their worry, and Damon couldn't blame them. Both teams were now playing with a fierce passion – neither team wanted to lose this night. He and Coach West had been right – the Diamondbacks were playing more roughly as the game continued and it took everything he had just to even stay on his own feet sometimes. Still, if he knew one thing for certain, he wasn't going to be the one to back down in this fight.

Damon was back on the field with a few minutes left of the third quarter. The cold had settled in but neither he nor the other players could feel it as their blood pumped through their veins. He could see the clouds of air as everyone caught their breath before he called the next play. The ground crunched a little under his feet as he shuffled his weight in preparation for the snap.

Moments later, the latest play was under way and Damon was scanning the field for an open man. He found his man all right, but unfortunately, so did the other team. He turned away from the scene of the player in brown and gold tackling his teammate to try and find another fellow Dragon who'd be free to make the catch. No one else was available though, and left with no other opening, Damon found himself rushing forward in between Vin and Riley, hoping that they'd be able to hold off the other guys to allow him to gain a few precious yards. As he passed, he noticed a slight scuffle going on on his right, but pushed it out of his mind as he continued to move forward. 'Just keep going, D. Keep going,' he kept thinking over and over to himself until he felt himself get tackled once more, protecting the ball in his arms as he came crashing down to the ground.

Another whistle was blown, and Damon found another flag being tossed to the ground. Immediately, he got up and looked around to see what was the matter. It didn't take him long to see that behind him to his right, Riley was on the ground holding his ankle while the referee was trying to break up the crowd from surrounding him.

Fire coursed through his veins as he saw the pain etched on Riley's face and heard the mocking coming from the Diamondback side of the field. With a signal to his teammates, they backed off to allow a couple of the trainers get Riley off the field after getting a quick assessment of his injury.

"Two minutes," he told his team shortly. "Two minutes and then we're done with the third quarter. Let's just get through this, and we can go from there," Damon rallied his team. Those two minutes came and went without a score change, and soon, Damon was racing off the field. "How are you feeling?" Damon quickly rushed over to Riley's side as soon as he was in the locker room.

Riley looked up to see his friend's concerned face and tried his best to grin – it came out as a grimace. "I don't know, D. The trainer thinks it's just a couple of bruised ribs and a messed up ankle. I'm fine to stay until after the game, but there's no way I can get back on that field tonight. We're lucky I'm the only casualty there is right now, what with how those guys are playing out there."

Damon nodded grimly. "Did they get you some pain medication?"

"You get yourself busted up and see if you can get by without meds."

Damon smiled a little.

"Tell Ana I'm all right?"

"Of course I'll let her know. What's more, I'll personally take out that D-back that got you on this bench in the first place. From what the guys told me, that kind of play ought to have gotten the guy evicted from the game and not just a five minute time out!"

"Easy, Damon," Riley said, trying to calm his friend down after seeing a dark gleam enter into his eyes. "I just planted my leg wrong is all."

"And the other player just happened to hit you in just the right way so that it would twist, right?" he added sardonically.

"He'll get what's coming to him, with your help or not," Riley said in a quiet tone. He tilted his head towards Coach West and the rest of the team, which had come in to check on their fallen teammate.

"Hey Riley, how are you feeling?"

The smile came a little easier on his face this time. "I'm hanging in there. Someone want to help me back out onto the bench so I can watch?" He watched as one of their trainers came over to do a little bit more evaluating as Damon led the rest of the team aside to discuss tactics for the last quarter. As much as he hated leaving the game, he knew that the team was in good hands. Riley half-listened as Damon gave his version of a pep talk, feeling the fiery energy coming off of him and his teammates in waves. He knew he wouldn't be let down.

- - -

Sharon watched silently for a moment as Ana and the other cheerleaders tried to pep up their side of the bleachers. The worried look on Ana's face betrayed her true emotions, however, and it wasn't until Damon came sprinting over to say something in her ear that Ana actually started smiling again. Whatever he'd told her must have helped because the anxious look in her eyes disappeared and was replaced with a fiery determination that she only knew came from Ana. That fire burned even brighter once Riley slowly came back up out of the locker room to the rousing cheers and standing ovation from his team and fans. Ana held her head high and proud, once again giving her all to her performance.

Still, her fire, as strong as it was, Sharon found herself admitting that it was no match for the inferno she saw in Damon's own eyes as he played. Even at this distance, she could see it, feel its tightly controlled but barely restrained energy. It was his energy that helped the Dragons to dominate the game the last twelve minutes' worth of gameplay that night. If she had thought the first three quarters were intense, it was nothing compared to what she was seeing now.

Damon was playing with a kind of natural grace that only came from months and years of hard work and dedication to his sport. The image of Riley on the ground and in pain was still etched in his mind as he called plays into action, his arm coming through time and time again to find his intended catcher. It didn't even matter that the other team was pulling out all the stops in a desperate attempt to slow the game back down to their tempo and work the ball in their favor. The Dragons were making all the calls those last few minutes and delivering in a way they hadn't yet all season.

And then the whistle blew.

28

Finally. It was over.

As the shrill echo of the whistle hung in the air for a few more precious moments, Damon found himself leaning over and resting his hands on his knees as he let out a sigh of relief. He finally allowed himself to take a look at the marquee for the first time since Riley had been injured.

48-14.

Shaking his head in disbelief, he found his face cracking open into a wide grin as he realized they'd won by leagues and was now witnessing the chaos take hold of the high school stadium. Riley was up on one leg, holding himself upright with a crutch yelling things Damon couldn't hear and giving high fives to his teammates as they came off the field. Coach West was still screaming, only this time with elation rather than frustration, and giving his boys some giant bear hugs while the cheerleaders did their thing a little further down as well. Family and friends were pouring from the bleachers to share in the celebration. Before he could spot anyone else though, a few of his fellow teammates finally came around, effectively making him a part of the party too.

He quickly lost count of how many people he greeted, how many people had congratulated him with a pat on the shoulder or otherwise. It was easy to get lost in the joyous feeling, even when he and his team shook the Diamondbacks' hands.

It was a quick moment with Riley, telling him they'd bring his usual from Marty's parlor before the injured player finally left to make his way to the hospital to have his leg looked at.

It was an even quicker moment with Coach. A quick hug with the older man saying how the next year was going to be a rebuilding one with Damon and the others moving on. Damon wisely kept his mouth shut on hearing the thick emotion in the older man's voice and seeing the proud tears in his eyes, opting to hug him again before turning to scan the crowd once more.

He felt a pair of arms encircle his legs first and looking down, he felt his smile grow wider. "There's my favorite sister in the world!" he announced as he swooped down to pick her up.

Ros threw her arms around his neck, giggling. "Yay Damon! You guys won!"

"That we did," he said as he drew Caleb over to give him a hug as well. "I'm so glad you guys were here to see it."

"As if we'd miss your last game," Caleb grinned before drawing away to give their parents a chance to say their congratulations.

After a few minutes of speaking, his family said their good nights and went on their way home as Ros was starting to get tired from all the excitement.

"Don't stay up too late, all right?" Mrs. Cardinet asked as she gave Damon one last pat on the cheek before leading the family over to the parking lot.

A quick glance around showed that some families were indeed leaving.

And then he spotted her, sitting on her own on the second row of bleachers a little bit away from him, taking in the scene in front of her and smiling a little to herself.

Damon's feet immediately started moving him forward towards Sharon.

Feeling his gaze on her, Sharon turned her attention to Damon as he took a few strides to the bleachers. Before he could make it to the stands though, Sharon watched as Kari chose just that moment to catch Damon by the arm and stall him. Knowing Ana's version of her attitude towards Damon, Sharon took interest in the interaction below her. From what she could tell, it looked like whatever she was pleading for was falling on deaf ears. Damon took her hand off his arm as gently as he could and kept shaking his head no, giving Kari an apologetic smile before continuing to make his way up the bleachers toward Sharon. With his back to the cheerleader, he missed the indignant look she shot Sharon's way. Instead of looking away though, Sharon kept her eyes locked with Kari's until Kari decided to just leave with a flip of her hair, stomping off towards the locker rooms.

Damon noticed the twinkle in Sharon's eyes and grinned when she patted the seat next to her left. "Thanks. You look amused."

"Just had an amusing sight is all."

"Oh? Of what?"

"Kari looking like she would kill me if she could."

Damon arched an eyebrow. "And this was amusing?"

"Oh come on. The poor girl obviously wants you."

"My status you mean. How'd you know this?"

"Give me some credit here," she said as she gave him a playful nudge. "I have eyes and ears, not to mention a verbal threat from her from a while ago."

"She what?" A spark of something turned on in his eyes, and he turned his gaze to try to spot the offending girl.

"Damon, don't," she said, drawing his attention back to her by physically turning his face back to hers with a touch of her gloved hand to his cheek. "She's not worth the trouble, and besides, I'm made of thicker skin than she'd believe. It's all right."

Damon sighed. "I don't take harm towards the ones I'm close to very well."

"Well that much was obvious, especially with what happened to Riley earlier. It's an admirable trait you have, surely, but trust me Damon. She was only trying to stake her claim and trying to get me to back off from spending so much time with you."

"But I like spending time with you," Damon pouted a little as he lifted an arm to wrap around her shoulders and give her a squeeze.

The smile on Sharon's face grew with the gesture. "And I like spending time with you too, which is why I can't and don't listen to or worry about Kari. There are plenty of other things to keep these brain cells of mine occupied."

An easy laugh came from Damon. "You are too much, Shar."

"And you wouldn't have me any other way," Sharon smiled.

"Nope, not at all," Damon agreed.

"Damon! Sharon!" Meet you at Marty's?"

The two looked down towards the field and spotted Vin and Damon nodded, giving Vin and his family a wave as they headed off the field.

"We better get going too then. Want a ride?" Damon asked as he stood up and offered Sharon help up as well.

"A ride would be great actually. My parents left right at the end of the game to beat the traffic and I figured I'd bum a ride home from someone."

"Well then give them a call while I go in to change and let them know that I'll take you to Marty's and drop you off afterward too if that's all right."

"Sounds like a plan," Sharon smiled as the two continued to walk hand in hand towards the guys' lockers. "Hey, and before I forget to say it, you guys did awesome out there tonight."

Damon shrugged but kept smiling. "The team pulled through. I couldn't have done it without them."

"Spoken like the true captain you are. You know, as little as I know about this game, I can't deny the energy that goes into it all or how exciting it is to watch you play your hearts out," Sharon stated, turning her head towards Damon.

"I don't play the sport just because I like to get thrown to the ground," Damon joked.

"Ahh yes, there is the high risk of injury too. It's painful enough watching how you play sometimes so I can only imagine how you guys feel. How are you feeling anyway? You took a handful of falls out there on the field."

He shrugged. "I'm all right. I might be a bit more sore than normal tomorrow, but it's a good thing we've got so much padding on to help against some of the injuries."

Sharon laughed. "Very true, but now you need to go get changed out of said padding. I don't think it'll be needed for any more injuries tonight at Marty's."

Damon laughed. "All right, I get it. Go call your parents and see what they say."

"Thanks, Damon," she smiled.

He gave her hand a last squeeze before turning to head inside, his spirits high for more than one reason that December evening.

29

The rest of the semester flew by and soon enough, Sharon's family was off to Colorado to meet with Kelly and her family.

Kelly waved a hand in front of Sharon's face. "Earth to Sharon! You're daydreaming on me again," she whined.

Sharon blinked and refocused on the present moment. "Huh? What'd you say?"

Kelly gave a dramatic sigh as she leaned back into the overstuffed chair she was in. "Seriously woman, I'd throw this cushion at you if you weren't holding that hot chocolate."

"Ahh, looks like I've found an effective shield then," came the cheeky reply as Sharon took a sip from the mug in her hands.

"You can't sit there all day long with the hopes of avoiding the inevitable. Plus we're hitting the slopes again. I don't think you've got enough hands to be able to ski and hold your mug at the same time."

"Seriously, with all the gadgets in this world, you'd think someone would have come up with a thermos to attach to your ski poles or something."

Kelly scoffed. "That just sounds like an accident waiting to happen right there." Sharon gave a small shrug and shifted a bit in her seat to get herself in a more comfortable position. "So really, what were you spacing out on me with or do I really need to ask?"

Sharon smiled again. "Do you really have to ask?"

Kelly gave another sigh. "I see how it is. Best friend here is getting replaced with a boy, granted the boy is hot, smart, talented, and makes you go all googly-eyed on me. I seriously don't know what you see in him," she teased.

"Do you want me to expand on your overly simplified list or not?"

"Sharon!" Kelly laughed. "You've gone all feisty on me! It's such a relief to get this back from you!"

"You say it like it's been missing for forever."

"Well, hasn't it?"

"It wasn't missing. It's just been laying dormant until now, when I'm most relaxed and at ease."

"Which means you've been stressing out more since I last saw you. Finals?"

Sharon nodded. "Are now done and over with and are hopefully good enough for the transcripts that are going out. How's your studying going?"

With a shrug, she replied, "All I can say is at least we have a couple weeks after vacation to study before finals happen for me. I'll take care of it then."

"Smartie pants," Sharon grinned, to which Kelly just rolled her eyes.

"So academics aside, is there anything else that pretty head of yours stressing out over?"

"Just those and college applications. I don't know Kelly. College is such a huge deal and it could make or break you, depending on where you end up. How is one to choose where to go?"

"Shar, it's what you make out of what life throws

at you that determines how you end up, and I know for a fact that no matter where you go, you'll make it just fine."

"And how are you so sure about that?"

"You're more than just surviving your senior year at a new high school – you're thriving. I mean look at you, you're practically glowing here with happiness."

"And I attribute that to being in the presence of my BFF."

"As flattered as I am with that comment, I know I don't deserve all the credit here. You're doing well for yourself Sharon, and there's no reason that shouldn't continue for you during college and beyond."

"Thanks Kelly, for everything," Sharon replied, beyond touched by her friend's kind words.

"Anytime, Shar. No matter where we end up, I will be there for you to lay it all out, the good and the bad."

"Here's to us and our friendship," Sharon said as she lifted her mug into the air and Kelly did the same.

"Ahh, so this is where you to went," Kelly's brother Wade said as he took the seat next to Kelly's in the bustling lobby of their lodge. "I should have figured you two would get something hot to drink after this morning's runs. How's the hot chocolate Sharon? Any good?"

"It's not the powdered kind, I can say that."

"Ahh, I'm sold. I'll be right back then."

After he had excused himself, Sharon turned back to Kelly. "He seems chipper and happy this morning."

"It probably means either of two things. Either he ended up not falling too much or too badly on the slopes so far today, or he's found some cute eye candy to work his charms on for the next few days while we're here."

"My bet?"

The two looked back at each other in the eye after giving Wade a quick glance. "Eye candy," came the response in unison, resulting in more laughter and a few glances to be made their way as the two continued to enjoy one another's company.

- - -

"Hey kids! Come downstairs for a little bit will you? The mail's here, and there's even something here for you too Ros," the Cardinet father called out.

Ros let out a squeal as she thundered down the stairs. "Something for me? Is it the doll Santa forgot to give me for Christmas?"

"Ros, you know better than to be ungrateful for everything else Santa gave you this year!" Mrs. Cardinet reprimanded as the little girl made her way into the dining room, followed closely by Caleb and Damon.

"Sorry mom," she pouted. "Does that mean I have to give back my toys from this year?"

Damon smiled and took the opportunity to pull lightly on his sister's ponytail. "Not this time. Santa gave you those toys as gifts, and didn't you know it's rude to return a gift?"

"Uh uh…"

"Well then, now you know. Santa gave you those presents for a reason. Just keep being the good girl you are, and Santa will bring you more things next Christmas, maybe even that doll."

"You think so?"

"Doesn't hurt to be nice," Mrs. Cardinet replied as she handed Damon a few packets that he quickly glanced over, seeing that they were all more college applications, and gave Ros the postcard from the pile still in front of her. "Here Ros. This one's for you."

The little girl took a seat on Damon's lap and gazed at the snowy white picture of the mountains. "Ooh, it's so pretty. Where is this?"

"Turn it over and let's find out," Damon suggested. When she did so, he pointed to the small print in the top corner. "It says here that it's a picture from the Rocky Mountains all the way in Colorado. You know where that is, right?"

"Yeah Ros. I showed you on the map when I was learning it in school a few weeks ago, remember?" Caleb asked, looking up from the card he'd gotten from an uncle.

Ros scrunched her face in concentration as she tried to remember that lesson. "Maybe. Can you show me again?"

Caleb nodded before pointing back to the postcard in her hand. "What does it say?"

She glanced down and frowned a little bit. "I don't know. I don't know all these letters yet. We only got through letter M before vacation started."

"Here. Let me help you this time and then we can go over your letters again upstairs, okay?" Damon asked.

Ros agreed and pointed to the first word. "Start here,"

Damon grinned. "All right. It says:

Dear Princess,

   How is your winter vacation going? Are you glad that you're spending a lot of time with your family and playing with your new toys? I imagine you are. Me, I'm having fun here skiing with my family and Kelly and her family, but I do miss you too. I'll see you soon though when I get back. Love, Sharon

   P.S. Give everyone in your family a big hug for me and a kiss on the cheek for Damon too. Happy New Year!

Mr. Cardinet gave a small cough. "Kiss on the cheek Damon? I don't remember reading that on the postcard."

"Must be the poor lighting conditions you've been complaining about lately," Damon joked even as he blushed a little.

"Come on Damon. Help me put this up on my wall," she said as she jumped off his lap and tugged on his hand to hurry him along, saving him from further teasing from his family.

30

Sharon was taking her time walking from her locker to her first class when she felt a warm hand gently take one of her arms and loop it within his. "Damon," she acknowledged, turning her head and giving him a warm smile.

"Sharon," he greeted back, an easy smile on his face matching her own. "Welcome back. Glad to see you back safe and sound. No broken bones it looks like."

"It helps that I've been skiing since I was a little kid. The mountains were so beautiful though. Have you ever gone?"

He shook his head. "To be honest? That is one thing that my family never got around to doing. My dad's job keeps him really busy, so the vacations we took were mostly to places we could drive away to for the weekend or a few days."

"So no snow then?"

"Never."

"That's so sad!" Sharon found herself exclaiming. "Looks like we'll have to remedy that somehow then."

Damon gave her a skeptical look. "Last I heard, there are no mountains high enough to have snow here. I should know. I've lived here all my life."

Sharon smiled back. "I'll think of something, don't you worry. I can't let you graduate high school without knowing about snow now, can I? That's like growing up not knowing how to ride a bike or swim or something."

"You make it sound like I've led a sheltered life," he teased.

The warning bell sounded through the halls at that point, and Sharon shook her head. "I'll come up with something," she repeated as Damon dropped her off at her first class. He just shook his head in reply before ducking into the room next door.

That Saturday though, Damon couldn't help but stare in wonder at the sight in front of him. All around him was a winter wonderland he'd never known about. Vaguely, he found himself getting out of the car and Sharon took his hand in hers as they made their way toward the main gate and paid.

"How'd you hear about this place?" he asked, looking around him in awe.

Sharon shrugged. "I just did a little bit of research. There are little places like this all around where I grew up, I knew there had to be someplace like it even here in the south. True, it's a bit of a drive to get here, and we had to wake up early for said drive, but-"

"But nothing, Shar! I just can't believe I never knew of this place any sooner. You're beyond awesome!" Damon let out, looking entirely like a little kid walking into his first candy shop and not knowing what to take in first. He couldn't help but stare in wonder, moving slowly in a circle to take in the snow all around him.

"Come on then," Sharon said, grabbing onto a hand and tugging onto it. "I'll race you to the slopes."

Damon gave a laugh as he jogged after her, having fun going down on the man-made snowy slopes in inner tubes as well as joining in a free for all snowball fight toward another side of the grounds. Sharon gave a laugh as Damon felt the cold, wet snowball she'd just thrown towards him leave its mark on his chest. With a roll of his eyes, he found himself stooping down to form another snowball when a small bundle knocked into him and caused him to fall back onto the snow covered ground. "Ros?" he asked, not believing his eyes.

"It's really snow Damon!" Ros was squealing as she jumped up from her tackle and began jumping up and down. "Snow, snow, snow!"

"Where'd you come from?" he tried to ask, but she was already up and running back towards Caleb with a snowball ready in her hand. A ways off, he spotted his parents and gave them a wave.

"As if I could just kidnap you without telling your family where I was taking you," Sharon smiled as she came closer. "Your mom mentioned they'd try to come as soon as your siblings were awake."

He raised an eyebrow at that. "So you let them sleep in and not me?"

"And pass up on the chance to have you all to myself without having to share? Yeah right," she replied back, a twinkle in her eyes.

Damon couldn't find the words to reply just that moment. He was already overwhelmed with his first time in the snow but adding to that her words… All he could do was stare at her openly, taking in her smiling, uninhibited self and wonder again at the effect she was having on him. He shook his head a little and sheepishly looked away.

"What? No witty remark? I hope that means I'm forgiven again for not being able to make it to the dance with you during winter break."

He shook himself out of his brief reverie and rested an arm around her shoulders, turning her so they could leave the snowball field and walk towards one of the booths that he'd spotted selling hot chocolate. "What's a high school dance compared to sharing an experience like this? I think you're trying to spoil me."

"Some people are worth it."

Damon looked down at Sharon again, trying to take her in this new light and gather the thoughts that were running freely in his mind. "You're different."

"In what way?"

"You're not holding back here," he gestured around them.

She shrugged. "I don't feel like I need to."

"But why? Why here? Why now?"

She gave him a thoughtful look as he ordered two hot chocolates and paid for them. She gratefully took one of the offered paper cups, and they walked over to a nearby bench. "Maybe it's because I'm realizing that I really don't need to hold back, not with you."

"But you were before."

She nodded, but didn't open her mouth to explain further. They each took a couple of silent sips of their drinks, watching as families all around them shrieked and squealed in the wintry wonderland around them.

A thought crossed his mind, and Damon opened his mouth before he could stop himself. "So Sharon, you still haven't answered me."

"Answered what?"

"I vaguely remember asking you some time ago if you want me to stop liking you."

It took her a few moments but a smile formed on her lips as soon as she recalled the memory and he was glad he hadn't had to remind her of what he was referring to. "Ahh… the mashed potatoes…"

He nodded. "Well?"

She grinned back at him. "Refresh my memory. What was the question?"

He rolled his eyes but found himself repeating the question anyway. "Do you want me to stop liking you?"

"And you are asking me this because…"

"Well, you've been very direct and open and honest with me today. Your answer could very well change the course of how things pan out…"

"Vague answer there, mister." He just shrugged and looked at her expectantly. She tried again, angling herself so she was facing him directly on the bench and he turned to mirror her position. "Damon, you're right. I realized a couple things while I was away for vacation, and part of all that is definitely why I am being very direct and open and honest with you."

"Because you trust me."

Sharon gave a nod of her head. "I do."

"And because you like me."

She grinned and didn't say anything for a few

moments, but a faint blush crept onto her cheeks anyway, betraying her feelings. "I will not deny that statement."

"So you don't want me to stop liking you?"

"No, I must confess I do not, if that's what you feel."

"Good," he replied, reaching out to take one of her hands in his. "Because I don't think I could have stopped even if you had asked me to."

She rewarded him with a full smile, one that matched the one he had on his face already. "You know, I'm really happy you asked me out before we vacation. I'm just sorry we couldn't go out more than the one time before I left."

"It's okay," he shrugged. "We can make up for the lost time. Like today," he grinned.

"Hey Damon! Can we go onto the ice now?"

Damon turned to see Caleb and Ros walking up to them with pleading looks on their faces. He turned back to Sharon with a questioning look even as he tugged her up off the bench. As the two started following his siblings out towards the rink, he couldn't help but wrap an arm around Sharon's shoulders and drawing her close. Even through their bundled clothing, each could feel the warmth of the other. "Thank you again for stealing me away while you could."

"Just as long as I don't have to share you all the time, I'll be fine," she smiled, wrapping one arm around his waist as well.

31

Ana came up to Sharon's locker, where she was organizing her things. "Someone's looking very thoughtful now," Ana remarked, taking in the other girl's pensive mood as she found the last notebook she needed and slammed her locker door shut.

"Hey Ana," she smiled as the two turned toward their last class, which they shared.

"Hey to you too. You alright?"

"As all right as can be I guess. You know, I knew that going out with Damon officially was going to cause some talk, and I guess I keep forgetting how small the high school is, but it's still a little weird sometimes."

"What? Are people giving you any trouble?" concern for both her friends showing as a small frown formed on her face.

Sharon gave Ana what she hoped was a reassuring smile. "Nothing that I truly can't handle on my own. People are just curious. I still haven't been the most forthright with my past you know."

"And you have your reasons. Speaking of which," she started as they took their adjacent seats with a minute to spare before the bell. "How are you holding up on that front?"

"Not bad," Sharon gave her a low reply, trusting Ana to understand.

"Have you said anything to him yet?"

Now Sharon looked away, giving a small sigh. "Not yet. How can I bring up something that has such bad feelings associated with it and taint this happiness I have now? Besides, it's in the past. It's done."

Ana gave a sympathetic smile. "All right, so perhaps now isn't the best time to bring it up, but you know you'll need to tell him, right?"

Sharon smiled a little and shrugged, truly unsure of that answer. She knew she had to be open with Damon, to let him know a bit of that part of her history, but as she told Ana, she just didn't want to bring up any more of those bad memories if she didn't have to. Thankfully, the bell chose that moment to ring, and their conversation took a break as both girls turned their attention to the teacher at the front of the room.

- - -

Later that night, as Sharon was working on her latest physics assignment, she heard her mom calling up to her to pick up the phone. "It's Kelly!"

Sharon hurried to turn her stereo down before grabbing the phone. "Kelly? What's up?"

"Hey Sharon! Oh nothing much. I know it's late and we both have homework to do so I'll keep it short. Did you get my package yet?"

"The books? Yeah, I actually just got it today. I still can't believe you finished those so quickly. How'd you manage that one?"

"I couldn't sleep on the plane ride back, so that took care of the first book. As for the rest, well, I'm not like you where I can just stop a good story in the middle. I had to keep going!"

Sharon laughed. "So now you're stuck on the same cliffhanger I am. I'm glad you like the series so far though."

"I love it! I may not be able to wait for you to send me the next one when it comes out. I may just end up buying it instead."

"Yay! Yet another vice I can share with you. What about you though?" she asked, changing the subject. "Did you get your CD's back yet?"

"You know, that was the other reason I was calling, to see if you had sent them back yet because I was thinking of using a couple of the songs for some projects I have going on here."

"I went to the post office after school sometime early last week. You still haven't gotten the package?"

"Naw uh. Did you track it?"

"I didn't think I had to. We never had issues in the past. Oh, I'm so sorry Kelly! I'll get you another copy of all of those."

"Don't worry about it, Shar. I'm sure they'll turn up eventually. And if not, then you can get me the music some other time."

"I still feel bad though."

"Well, we'll wait a couple more days and then go from there. Sound good?"

"Just let me know."

"Of course. Anyway, that was it. I'll talk to you later?"

"Fine, make me go back to homework," she laughed before they each said their goodbyes and hung up. Sharon turned her stereo back up and sat back at her desk. It took her a couple minutes to settle down though. Something about that conversation bothered her, and she had a vague, bad feeling about things. 'Why wouldn't she have gotten that package? Mail gets lost every day, but is that enough reason to just brush it off? Well, no use worrying now. You'll pay her back when you see her again at spring break…'

And with that, Sharon forced herself to refocus her attention to the problems literally in front of her so she could finish her homework.

32

Ana eyed the couple across the table from her and couldn't help but grin. After Damon had told her the news that he'd finally asked Sharon to be his girlfriend, she'd found the two had been inseparable ever since. Sharon was sitting cross-legged in her chair, leaning over the table and Damon had scooted his chair as close to her as possible, wrapping his left arm around her shoulders as they each studied for their respective classes. Sharon was punching away some numbers on her calculator, getting her physics homework done. Damon was surprisingly focused on his homework for government class.

"You know," Ana started quietly, as they were in the library. "I think Sharon's a good influence on you, Damon. You were never this focused when we studied before."

The teen had looked up from his work to grin over at Ana and Riley, whose head was currently down on his arms. "Yes, I was, what are you talking about?"

Ana arched an eyebrow at him. "Oh really? I don't think you were ever able to sit for over two hours before without taking a break."

Now he looked over in surprise. "Has it been that long already?" He glanced about, trying to look for a clock. "I didn't even notice."

"You looked comfortable enough," she teased.

Sharon glanced over then. "And he's doing double duty, multi-tasking and keeping me warm as well," grinning over to Damon before he gave her a quick kiss on the cheek.

A faint blush crept up into Sharon's cheeks as she turned back to the equations in front of her. Damon gave her one last squeeze before he also turned back to the text in front of him.

A couple hours later, the four of them were walking downtown after having spent some time at Marty's after they were done studying. Dessert and a few minutes' worth of goodbyes later, the two couples parted ways, Damon steering Sharon by the hand to walk further down the street with him. "So what are you doing after school tomorrow?" Damon asked Sharon.

"Babysitting," she replied.

"Oh? Where at?"

"Your place."

He looked up, startled. "Huh?"

She chuckled at the expression on his face. "Your mom asked me to come over after school again so she can run errands without Ros or Caleb around."

He smiled easily now, the initial surprise gone. "That's great. You think you'll be staying for dinner then?"

"I don't think so. I'll only be over for a couple of hours until your mom comes back."

"Oh… Well, see if you can wait until I get home about 5:30 or so."

She glanced over, a suspicious look on her face. "Why?"

He smiled back an innocent smile. "It's a surprise."

"And should I trust this surprise?"

"Why not?"

"If I recall correctly, the first time you had a surprise for me, I ended up helping feed the frosh class to help boost school spirit, remember?"

"But that wasn't a surprise! I asked you to do it, and you agreed."

"You asked me to come to school early, not to feed anyone," she clarified.

"Point taken, but will you still stay on until I get home?"

"I don't know..." she hesitated. "Unless there was a really, really good reason for me to stay..."

"There is, I promise you."

"You haven't broken any promises yet…"

"And if it is in my power, you never will get any broken promises from me ever."

Sharon pulled them to a stop, causing him to turn back to face her one on one. "That's a tall order, Damon. Are you really up to that?"

"You have my word," he readily replied, letting her see the sincerity in his eyes as he said so.

Sharon was silent a few extra moments, gazing into his eyes and then she nodded. "I'll have to put trust in your word then."

"So does that mean you'll stay tomorrow?"

She grinned as they started walking again. "If both our parents say yes, then yes, I'll stay for a little bit."

The next day, Damon stayed true to his word. As he walked Sharon out to her car after dinner with the family, she gave him a quizzical eye. "You were quiet today at dinner. What's on your mind?"

He turned to Sharon and gave a small smile as he leaned against her car. "Something my dad told me the other night."

"Oh?" She tilted her head to one side, waiting for him to continue.

"Yeah. He just asked if I was sure."

"About…"

"About this." He took a hand out of his pocket and pulled something out. As she stepped closer to see, she noticed that it was his class ring, and it was looped through with a delicate chain. She turned back to Damon's face, a puzzled look in her open gaze. "I thought it was the silliest tradition for a while until recently, when I realized that I can be a bit old-fashioned at times too. Sharon, I am serious about you, about us, and I was wondering if you would honor me by wearing my class ring."

She reached up a hand and gently let a finger trace the ring in his palm, a smile coming across her face as she took in the dragon emblem on the side. "Damon, I am sincerely touched. Are you sure though? I know that this symbolizes a lot for you." He nodded, suddenly finding his throat too tight for any more words as he gazed at this woman in front of him at sunset. "Then yes, I do accept." She allowed him to lift up the necklace and stepped in close so he could fasten the clasp behind her.

Rather than step away though, he kept his arms encircled lightly around her waist and drew her forward for a sweet kiss. "Thank you," he whispered. "You have no idea how much I care for you, how much I love you right now."

She smiled. "I think I have an idea," she answered with another kiss.

33

The spring carnival was in full swing by the time Damon and Sharon arrived hand in hand. The streets leading to the community park had all been full, and they'd had to park further away than expected, but with the weather being as perfect as it was for that spring afternoon, they didn't mind the walk.

The end of school was almost upon them, a mere couple weeks away and with it, the last of their finals. For now though, the whole community came together to celebrate spring, and the two joined their friends at various rides and games. Life had been a blur since Damon had given Sharon his ring what with college visits and classes and his student government responsibilities. And through it all, they did everything together, supporting each other. Even Mr. Cardinet was softening even more to the girl on Damon's arms. Yes, he had his reservations – his boy still had his whole life ahead of him, and he didn't want him to feel restricted in any way, least of all by a girl. Still, he supposed it was for their best for now as the two seemed to make each other better. For the meantime.

Sharon excused herself for a moment to use the restroom, leaving Damon in line with their friends at one of the food booths. "Get me some popcorn?" He nodded, and they shared a brief kiss before she moved toward the restrooms. When she exited a few minutes later, she scanned the crowd and realized that Damon and her friends had already left the food booth. Her eyes continued to scan the crowd when she felt an icy chill wash over her. Something felt wrong, and it wasn't until she spotted him that she understood why.

Before she could process what she was doing, her feet flying in Damon's direction, a terrified scream tearing out of her throat.

Damon quickly turned toward where Sharon was running toward him, arms opening to catch her even as his mind processed the terror on her face. "Wha-" he started to question until his mind registered the sound of a gunshot erupting from somewhere nearby. As if in slow motion, he watched as Sharon's body jerked just in front of his own, shielding him from a bullet that had been intended for him. Now he was the one rushing forward to catch Sharon just before she could crumple all the way to the ground, blood already seeping through the back of his letter jacket that she'd been wearing. He looked up and saw another male about their age standing about ten feet away, gun still raised and pointed in his direction, a finger poised and ready to pull the trigger. A cold, steely look was on the guy's face, a look of jealousy and anger the like of which Damon had never seen before. Before he could process anymore, the guy acted as if he were going to pull the trigger again, and that's when Vin and Riley both came to the rescue, knocking the gun loose and tackling him to the ground.

"Ana, 911, now!" Riley was yelling to his

girlfriend even as he and Vin continued to try to contain the squirming man under them, though for two football players, the struggle wasn't too much of a big one. Screams were echoing nearby, and people were running in all directions, trying to get away.

And just like that, the world sped up to real time again. "Sharon?" Damon vaguely noticed the shakiness to his voice as he tried to apply pressure to her back. "Are you okay?" He tried to work her arms so she could remove the jacket but he quickly noticed it was causing her more pain, her skin quickly paling with the shock and loss of blood, and so he just held her tight, pressing around her wound to stop the flow as best as possible. "Stay with me, Sharon."

"I'm sorry," she whispered, tears flowing even as the pain threatened to overwhelm her.

"Shh, just focus on me. You'll be okay, got it? You're going to be okay."

She tried to nod her head and ended up closing her eyes a moment, trying to focus on his calming words and presence even as the sound of sirens began to filter through the haze. "Get Ana to explain to you, okay?"

"Ana?" Damon's curiosity was piqued but he just accepted it for now as she nodded again and closed her eyes again in pain.

Voices around her seemed to be coming further and further away. Another set of arms began assessing her back before she felt herself being lifted up onto a platform to begin rolling away.

Hours later, Sharon found herself in a hospital

room recovering from the surgery where doctors had removed the bullet and tried to piece together the shredded tissue. "She's lucky," she kept hearing, over and over as the providers and nurses kept coming in to check on her. Her parents had come as soon as they'd heard and hadn't left her side since she'd left the operation room. The police officers had said the same thing as soon as they heard she was awake enough to give her account. Sure, she was lucky to be alive, lucky that the wound hadn't hit any major organs, lucky that it'd only been one gunshot, lucky that her friends had prevented him from firing anymore... But then she'd had to explain what she'd seen, explain who the gun wielder was in relation to her life, explain the threat that he'd been to her and her loved ones and the reason for their moving far away to here.

During the interview, one of the officers pulled out a torn piece of paper bearing her address on it, saying it had been in the gunman's pocket when they got to the scene. Sharon immediately identified it as originally part of the package she had sent her friend, the one that had gone missing with the returned CDs months ago. And it was seeing that envelope that caused Sharon to shut down. By the time the officers had left, with reassurance that the guy had been apprehended and was locked away in the meantime, she had made her decision. She turned to her parents and discussed that she didn't want to see anyone else again from the school. To protect those she had come to care for deeply, she would keep away. Nothing they said could dissuade her otherwise, and in the end, they had to accept her wishes, going so far as to go downstairs to where Ana was waiting to give her the ring that had proudly hung from their daughter's neck until that day in order that she give it back to Damon. Why Ana was there and not Damon didn't seem to register on anyone's mind until a few days later, but in the end, Sharon had already guessed why.

When Sharon had left on the ambulance, Ana had quickly told Damon what Sharon had shared with her earlier in the year regarding her past, how her last boyfriend had become possessive and abusive to the point where he had snapped and physically hurt her after he'd found her at Kelly's house without his knowing where she'd be. Kelly had tried to protect her friend but was just shoved against a wall for her efforts and was unable to do anything but watch as he had all but dragged Sharon out of her house. No one could have guessed Patrick's true nature until that point, though looking back, there had been warning signs of his possessive, abusive nature, but his anger left tell-tale marks, beating her too to the point where she had had to be admitted to the hospital.

Of course, he'd tried to say he was sorry, apologize and claim that it was all an accident and misunderstanding, but the damage had been done, and it wasn't like the bruises on her face weren't there.

Restraining order filed, her parents had taken the first chance out when her dad had applied for a position at another location, landing them in this town.

Even as Ana was finishing the story, both

suddenly noticed Mr. Cardinet nearby, who had come to search for his son after ensuring the rest of the family had been fine in the carnival. The look on his face let them know he had heard enough, and in the end, he had just given a sigh and said, "No more."

Damon felt absolutely torn. Shortly after the incident, his father had all but banned Damon from seeing Sharon again. "For his own safety and good," was the reason. There would be no questions. Damon at first couldn't believe it. "I'll see her at school. We can talk then, figure things out."

But the days kept passing, and there was still no sign of Sharon coming back. Belatedly, he heard that she was finishing her classwork remotely. Finals came and went too, and he started to lose hope that he'd ever see her again, even after Ana had given back his ring. "She has to come to graduation," he tried to reason with her and their friends.

But graduation itself came and went, and along with it an awkwardness when her name was not announced, though her name was still printed in the program. It was as if she had completely disappeared.

Damon was still puzzling things over when, on a whim, he decided to go back to the high school a few days after graduation and before summer session started to see if he could find someone to talk to about all of this. He never expected to see Sharon again there, but he did.

Coming up the stairs and rounding the corner, he immediately froze once he noticed that Sharon was there at her locker, slowly taking things out and placing them in a shoulder bag. No one else was around, and so he took a few moments to just watch as she carefully took down the pictures from inside her locker door and place them in a folder. He was aware that she was moving slowly, whether it was from the physical pain she was probably still recovering from or the emotions he could almost imagine weighing her down, he couldn't tell. She touched one that had been of the two of them at senior ball – how long ago that felt right then. Even from where he stood a few feet away, he could hear her sigh, and he watched as she closed her eyes to lean against the adjacent locker for a moment.

Steeling himself for just a moment longer, Damon took his first step into the hall, and the sound echoed in the otherwise empty hallway, causing Sharon to spin around quickly. Once she had registered his presence, she just as quickly turned away, though not quick enough for him to not catch the pain in her eyes.

He stopped a few lockers away from her and watched silently as she moved a little quicker to empty out her locker of the rest of her belongings. Most of her books and notebooks had already been removed so she could study from home, but there were still the rest of her paperwork and reports that still needed to be cleaned out too. Once that was empty, she turned back to the locker door and removed the last of the pictures, taking their senior ball photo down last. With a final glance through her locker, she slipped her bag off its hook so she could shut the door one last time. Rather than shoulder her bag though, she let it drop to the ground and finally faced Damon head on.

He took the sight in and felt his heart ache. Gone was the open, trusting look to her eyes. The strength he had noticed the first day they had met was gone too. Here was someone who had withdrawn deep into herself, and it hurt him more than he realized to see her like that.

"You forgot this." He broke the silence and fished in his pocket to take out the ring that she'd returned.

"I can't, Damon," she whispered, dropping her gaze and looking away.

"Why? What aren't you telling me?"

"Please, Damon. Just let this be."

"Let what be? Sharon, you just disappeared! Ros and Caleb keep asking me how you are. We've all missed you these last few weeks. We thought for sure you'd be there at graduation and then you weren't. I've missed you so much," the emotion running thick in his voice as he continued. "Sharon, just because your ex was psycho doesn't mean you needed to hide away forever. He's locked up – he's not going anywhere near you again."

He caught the flinch in her expression and took a step forward in an automatic response to try and comfort her. "Please don't."

"Why not?"

"Because!" She finally looked at him, anguish in her eyes.

"Because why?" He took another step forward.

"Because it doesn't matter, not anymore!" she exclaimed forcefully. She took a deep breath before continuing. "Look, you're going away for college, you're going to move on, you'll forget all about me, and it's better this way." She paused, closing her eyes. "The scene plays over and over in my head, Damon. I can't help but keep thinking that somehow, some way, I could have prevented all of this from happening."

"Sharon, listen, I know you're going through a lot right now, you're still healing, but I don't like how I'm not sure what's in your head right now. I don't like how I've just been completely shut out."

She shook her head. "I don't want to hold you back. I refuse to hurt you or anyone else, especially since this is all my fault. I just can't do that to you. No more."

Damon exhaled, the two last words ringing in his head. "You sound like my dad."

And just like that, he could almost see the curtain coming across her features as she turned away again and he could no longer look into her eyes.

"You've talked to him, yet I haven't heard once from you this entire time." The accusation hung in the air between them. "Why are you shutting me out?"

"He's a good man, and he means well. He wants to make sure you stay safe and on your path. I agree with him."

"Sharon?" He couldn't help the pain from escaping in his voice as he realized just how much things were out of his control. "What did he say to you?"

She just shook her head. "It doesn't matter. Just… It's time for me to go." She bent down and picked up her bag and walked around Damon, not once looking back up to his face.

She'd walked a few steps away when he asked, "So that's it? Just like that?" Her steps faltered to a stop, but she didn't turn around. "Am I ever going to see you again?" The last question was spoken in a whisper, but it pierced her just the same.

Fearing that she'd regret down the road what she was doing, Sharon spun around and quickly closed the distance between the two. With a fierceness he didn't know she had, she hugged him tight even as his mouth moved to cover hers in a kiss and his arms were reaching around to embrace her. He was just becoming aware of the tears slipping down her face when she tore herself away. "I'm so, so sorry," she whispered, and with that, she was running down the hall and stairs and out of the building.

Damon found that he couldn't move, his mind still trying to process exactly what had just happened.

EPILOGUE

Three months later…

Kelly blinked her eyes open. Something was up and she instinctively turned around in her bed to look for Sharon. She didn't find her best friend sleeping in bed, however. She was instead peering through the curtains of their hotel window, a hand drawing it to one side just enough so both eyes could see out. "Sharon?" she asked sleepily.

"Mm hmm?" came a soft reply.

"Is something wrong?"

"No."

"Are you sure?" she asked, unconvinced.

Sharon nodded imperceptibly to herself. "Just watching the sunrise."

Somewhere in the back of her mind, Kelly groaned and wondered what the girl was doing up so early. Still, she just found herself stating, "The sun rises every day, you know."

Sharon stayed quiet for a few moments and Kelly was beginning to think that something was definitely wrong and she was about to get out of bed herself when Sharon turned around, smiling a little as she dropped the curtain back, leaving the room dark once more. "Yes, I suppose it does," she finally answered as she settled herself back into bed. "Thanks for reminding me."

Kelly couldn't think of a reply but really found that there was no need for one. Whatever had gone on through Sharon's mind just then, she knew it had to be good because moments later, her best friend was sleeping easily. No tears, no sighs…

Kelly smiled a little before settling back onto her pillow. They still had half the country to see, and she already knew that they'd be full of fun and adventures. High school and all of its drama and pain were finally settling in the past where they belonged.

IN GRATITUDE

For those of us who have faced abuse, or are continuing to do so, know that you are not alone. I honor you for your journey, and bless you.

Also, my sincerest thanks to you for taking your time to read through my first serious attempt at fiction. I would greatly appreciate it if you took a moment to leave an honest review on Amazon and share with others via social media:

http://www.amazon.com/dp/

ABOUT THE AUTHOR

M. A. VALDELLON is a dreamer at heart.

When she's not immersed in the literary world, she can often be found playing and creating with crystals and music, cuddling with her furry loved ones, enjoying hot chocolate, and mentoring students and patients on their eyes and health in the Bay Area, California.

With four books already published and at least three more on the way, M. A. is certainly keeping herself out of trouble, but is not too busy as to be unavailable. You can contact her by email directly on her website, http://melissavaldellon.com/, and she will personally get back to you shortly.

Her next fiction, *Fairy Tales*, will be released February 2018.